The Double Dilemma

Lynn Shurr

A Wings ePress, Inc.
Historical Fiction Novel

Wings ePress, Inc.

Edited by: Jeanne Smith
Copy Edited by: Joan C. Powell
Executive Editor: Jeanne Smith
Cover Artist: Trisha FitzGerald-Jung

All rights reserved

Wings ePress Books
www.wingsepress.com

Copyright © 2020 by: Lynn Shurr
ISBN-13: 978-1-61309-576-8
ISBN-10: 1-61309-576-7

Published In the United States Of America

Wings ePress Inc.
3000 N. Rock Road
Newton, KS 67114

What They Are Saying About The Double Dilemma

"Shurr is a wonderful storyteller."

—The Romance Studio

"Very easy read, well written, combined with conflict, believable plots and secondary characters that make the story come alive."

—Janes Lange, *Romances, Reads and Reviews*

"I love the picture the author paints of the town and the way of life, and the characters are strong and interesting.

—Joan Conning Afman, Author of *The Cheetah Princess*

"Lynn Shurr breathes life into the characters and allows each turn of the page to lead up to a pleasurable ending."

—Cherokee *Coffee Time Romance and More*

"I love how deep and well-written the characters are."

—Juliette Brandt *Paperbacks and Frosting*

"You can count on Lynn Shurr to deliver interesting characters and great romance."

—A.C. Mason, author of *Deadly Bayou*

Dedication

In honor of Jane Austen and her *Northanger Abbey*.
With a nod to Shakespeare for his love of using twins
in his comedies.

* * *

***The progeny of Pearce and Flora Longleigh,
Duke and Duchess of Bellevue,
as recorded in the family Bible***

- James Logan Longleigh, Storm Cloud, born in the Ohio Territory, April 12, 1784?
- Thalia Amabel Full Moon Woman Longleigh, b. March 1, 1785
- Iris Emily Doe Eyes Longleigh, b. October 16, 1787
- Twins, Calliope Constance Corn Tassel & Clio Judith Small Turtle, b. June 22, 1789
- Joshua William Big Paw Longleigh, b. January 24, 1791
- Jason Samuel Benjamin Rattler Longleigh, b. January 24, 1792
- Pandora Jane Black Wing Longleigh, b. September 15, 1794
- Euphemia Dorcas Little Dove Longleigh, b. December 31, 1795
- Justinian Giles White Bull Longleigh, b. July 10, 1800

And all made the lives of their parents very interesting.

One

Bellevue Hall

North England, 1807

"We simply must marry twins because *we* are twins!" Lady Clio Longleigh tilted her head in that stubborn manner her mother, the Duchess of Bellevue, knew only too well.

Her identical but somewhat milder sister, Calliope, echoed her sentiment. "Yes, we do not wish to be parted by marriage and want our spouses to be sensitive to our feelings."

Standing by the fireplace mantel and soaking up most of the heat in the drafty, high-ceilinged drawing room of Bellevue Hall, their elder brother, James raised his dark eyebrows. "Surely, Mama, you are bringing out two of the silliest chits of the Season."

That earned a tut-tut from Lady Flora, the duchess. "Your sisters are very young and somewhat impractical, but certainly not silly. They will not turn eighteen until the end of June and perhaps are not ripe enough yet to go up to London this year."

She calmly poured three cups of tea for herself and her daughters. A smirk formed on James' sculpted lips as his sisters began to protest. He already sipped the Scotch whisky he'd grown to love while spending time at his estate in Scotland for the hunting and fishing, though the hour was only four of the clock on a dreary, damp, and chill February day in the north of England. Having reached his majority and being the family heir, he did what he pleased in a manly manner.

"Oh, no! We are quite ready to come out into society. Do not leave us at Miss Stilton's Academy for Young Ladies another term. Please!"

Lady Flora fixed each cup to their liking and passed the steaming beverage around. She inhaled the aroma of fine Darjeeling and warmed her hands at the same time. "James, please sit down. You are blocking the warmth of the fire."

Tall and stalwart of build like his father, he could stand in the way of many things if he wanted. Obedient to his mother's wish despite his size, he sank into an armchair and raised his feet to an ottoman.

Lady Flora continued to ponder the problem as if taking her young daughters very seriously. "The trouble with wanting to marry twins is finding a pair suitable to wed. Such births are rare and among the ton with its low rate of reproduction, even more scarce. I know of only two, Lord Blandon and his brother, Chester, and the Brompton brothers. The Bromptons are older than I, not that their age would impede a marriage necessarily, but they are quite unattractive and given to bad habits. Both have had two wives already. As for Lord Blandon, he is currently widowed, has gotten his heir, and shows more interest in spending time with Chet than finding another bride. Personally, I would not want to wed any of them."

"You've always said you never desired any man but Papa," Callie recalled.

"True, very true," the Duchess admitted. "But, Blandon and the Bromptons hold little appeal for any female. I cannot think of any others."

"I can."

The wide, brown eyes of his sisters turned toward James. So like the Duchess, being petite and curly-headed but dark, not fair of complexion and hair, they riveted their gaze upon him. Then Clio said, "He is teasing us as he always did in the nursery."

"Not so. I have a tale to tell." James left his chair and straddled the ottoman, allowing the fire to backlight his broad-shouldered body, and the branch of candles on the tea table to cast eerie shadows on his bronzed face with the small scar high on one cheekbone.

A gust of cold air announced the arrival of his father, Pearce Longleigh, Duke of Bellevue, as the man entered the room from the unheated hallway and closed the door behind him. "I hear I am in time for a story. Allow me to get a warming brandy before you begin."

Despite England being at war with Napoleon Bonaparte, the duke often stated that he saw nothing wrong with drinking spirits smuggled from France with no taxes paid to either government.

James was rather proud of his extraordinary father, though others might deem him old-fashioned, eccentric, and somewhat dangerous. Droplets of moisture bedewed his iron gray hair worn back in a long queue as if he still lived in the previous century. He dressed in that manner, too, favoring a greatcoat and knee breeches over tight pantaloons like the ones his son wore. Having gone out for a vigorous ride despite the foul weather, he had denied himself a lace cravat and the same touch at his cuffs.

The coming of dark and the lowering weather brought him home in a timely manner to sit beside his tiny wife who kept her curls a lovely shade of blonde no matter what her age and her complexion a flawless white, a contrast to his copper skin. Priding himself on the endurance and heartiness of his Shawnee Indian heritage, he refused to allow a bit of rain to keep him from getting out of the house and into the woods of his estate on any day. They were quite the parental pair.

"Tea first to warm you, my darling." Lady Flora pressed a fragile china cup into his big hand. She'd made it very sweet as he enjoyed it.

"I believe brandy would do that as well, but I would never refuse aught offered by your lovely hands." He kissed his wife's fingertips and made his children cringe. Jolly that their parents doted on each other, James thought, but their open displays of affection often embarrassed their many offspring. Helping himself to several small sandwiches, a few cakes, and a tartlet to tide him over until supper, the duke settled in to hear the tale.

"If we are finally ready," James said.

"We've been waiting," his sisters replied, not quite in unison. "Are these twins handsome and titled?" Clio asked immediately. "Not that they would have to be."

"Are they intelligent and kind?" Callie inquired. "Because that is most important."

Exasperated, James answered, "I do not know how to judge a man's looks with the eyes of a woman and did not linger with them long enough to say if they were kind. One has a title and both seemed intelligent. Now, might I move along?" They nodded, their black curls bobbing.

"Dodging Bonaparte's armies, I returned home from my studies in Germany by way of the Netherlands this time around. I boarded a merchant ship attempting to make its way to our shores despite the little emperor's orders."

"A smuggler do you mean?" the duke interrupted.

"Whatever you wish to call it! We entered the cold and choppy Channel, and all went well until one of Boney's privateers spotted us as we neared the coast of England and drove us south out of our way, causing us to miss the mouth of the Thames. Nelson might have destroyed the French fleet at Trafalgar, but the remnants still roam our sea. Both ships ran very swiftly in the ensuing chase. Suddenly, a bonfire blazed forth from a coastal cliff as if beckoning to us. Swearing our pursuer would not have his cargo or send us to the bottom, our captain made for a narrow cove intending to ground his craft if he must. Armed and on deck in case we were boarded, all of the crew as well as myself felt a great relief when a cannon began to fire seaward from the cliffs above. Some loyal and doughty Englishman had prepared against a French invasion and drove our enemy limping away with a hole in his mainsail and several smashed spars."

"You did not tell us this until now!" Lady Flora exclaimed. Her frightened gray eyes met ones very like her own in James' dark visage. Storm Cloud, the Shawnee had called him as an infant because of them.

"I did not want to worry you, Mama. Here I sit safe and sound. To proceed. We did come too close to the shore and fetched up on a bar of shingle, our ship as easy to pick off as a fat sea turtle on a beach if the gun should swivel our way. Fortunately, we soon saw a torch-lit procession making its way down the cliff to assist us. Led by a brute of a man with a missing eye, his minions soon helped us ashore and escorted us upward to a castle, a survivor from medieval times and so much a part of its rocky perch it seemed to grow directly from the bones of the earth." James squinted one eye, leaned forward, and leered at his sisters.

"Like *The Castle of Otronto*," Callie breathed.

James sat bolt upright. "For heaven's sake, Mama, have you been letting them read those Gothic horrors?"

Before Lady Flora could answer, Clio said, "No, we pass them around at night along with a candle at Miss Stilton's Academy. Each person must read at least one page aloud. If the matron hears us, the book will be confiscated and the person holding it punished. It's a wonderful game. I did three pages before passing it on. So did Callie because we are braver than most. The story is quite delicious."

"There is no harm in it, James. Why dear Horatio, though Walpole preferred to go by Horace, wrote quite an innocent and chivalrous tale. He kindly autographed a copy for me when I visited Strawberry Hill, and I have it still in our library."

Frustrated by interruptions and asides, James demanded, "Do you want to hear *my* story or not?"

"Yes! Yes!"

"We entered the old bailey through a raised portcullis and marched on to the great hall. Inside, a fire burned in an enormous hearth, but the furnishings appeared to be as ancient as the house, great blocky carved chairs and chests. Moldering tapestries covered the stones of the walls. No woman's touch softened that hall the way Mama made my Castle Laughlin pleasant and inhabitable. An older man sat in one of those kingly chairs and on either side of him, two young men, his sons by their resemblance to him, but I had to look twice at each because they could not be told apart. 'Welcome to the

Serpent's Mouth,' our host greeted." James lowered his voice making it more sinister and gravelly.

Callie sucked in her breath. Clio said, "But were the sons handsome?'

"I thought that did not matter, little sister. However, I can say both were about my height and well made. Blue eyes, hair a dark brown, shaggy, not stylishly cut at all, though they made a pretense of side whiskers." James ran a hand over his carefully cropped and coiffed head and shook his head, allowing one artfully placed curl to drop onto his forehead.

"Not everyone is a dandy, son," the duke had to mention.

"Being current with the times does not make one a dandy, Papa. No one calls me that and is allowed to get away with it."

"Good," said the duke, satisfied with his heir's masculinity.

"As I was saying, they were dressed decently enough but very plainly as if they'd never been to London or seen a good tailor. The captain and I were offered dinner in the hall at a trestle table while the crew went to the kitchen. Hearty food: game stew with root vegetables, fresh bread, sausages, red wine aplenty, and nuts, apples, a good cheese, and custards for our pudding. Mama, you would have remarked on the lack of salad and more delicate offerings."

"No woman's touch, as you said," she answered.

"More about the young men, please," Clio insisted.

"Not much more to say. They were cordial and seemed glad of some company other than that of their rather dour father. We played chess after the meal. One son won, one lost. I took the father easily and pocketed a small wager."

"Intelligent, as least one of them is." Callie bit into an apricot preserve tart rather too exuberantly and the crust flaked over the bodice of her high-necked, pale gray woolen gown enlivened by pale blue piping. Her sister wore the same but edged in cherry. She brushed the crumbs from her bodice.

"Nibble, please nibble, if we are invited to take tea while in the city," her mother corrected.

James gave a world-weary sigh. "Both performed well at the game, but I gathered they were so used to playing each other they did not anticipate my fresh moves. After, I was escorted to a room in their tower, and though it was rather cold and damp, I slept well enough under a mound of covers. In the morning, boats were put out to tow our ship from the bar, and the captain left an exceedingly generous parting gift of his wares for the help. He appeared to have some familiarity with the cove and indeed it did resemble a serpent's mouth, wide at the head, then narrowing and twisting as it neared the beach. The castle sat on the highest pinnacle but a great marsh swept away to south of the place. No other adventures occurred, and here I am at home for the time being."

"You left out a great deal," Clio chided.

"Did I?" Again, he raised his brows and cast an arch look at his sisters. Clio seized a small, iced cake and lobbed it at her brother. He caught it handily and gobbled it down. "Thank you, sister, I was a tad hungry after all this talking."

"I know we are *en famille*, but do not make me send you back to Miss Stilton—if she would have you again—for further polishing," the duchess admonished.

"What were their names, their age and ranks?" Clio said, largely ignoring her mother.

"Let me see if I recall." James put a hand to his chin and pretended to ponder. "Ah yes, the old man claimed to be Phineas Hardacre, Marquess of Blackwater. Evidently, he had some spare titles lying about and introduced his first born as Viscount Marston, given name, Gareth or was that Tristan, the other son? About my age, a trifle younger, perhaps. They dressed similarly and milled about the hall sporting with their many hounds before we settled down to a quiet game of chess. I could not keep track of them."

"They are fond of dogs, then. Which did you say bested you at chess?" Callie persisted.

"Can't really say."

"Oh, forget the chess and the dogs, Callie. If one of us were to marry Blackwater's heir, we would outrank our sister, Thalia, who has already wed an earl. Recall how she always had to be the queen when we played at dress-up, and we were only her ladies in waiting." Clio clapped her hands together and not simply to warm them.

"Actually, Queenie turned out rather well now that she has Danelagh to keep her in line," James reflected.

"A very stalwart man," his father approved.

"We would not immediately precede her as the heir is currently a viscount. Sister Iris is also married to a viscount and will become a countess, but she was always been kind to us so I do not mind whatever title she has." Callie twined a curl around her finger thoughtfully.

"Do not fiddle with your hair, dear," her mother said.

"Well, we were sent off to that dreadful boarding school simply because Thalia's governess found us too hard to handle as she groomed our sister to perfection. I can and do hold that against her." Clio's stubborn lower lip poked out.

"Don't let any man see that expression or you will never wed," her mother advised. "Your schools were dreadful because you made them so, but I see they did teach you the precedence of titles."

"That's all the other girls spoke of in the last year, dreadfully boring." Callie picked up a cake and nibbled it like a very small mouse, either obeying her mother or mocking her, always hard to tell with the quiet one. "I think it very unfair that a younger son gets nothing and the elder all, like James."

"Do you think these young men will be in London for the Season so that I might inspect them?" the duchess addressed her son. "I do not recall ever having heard of the Marquess of Blackwater, and I know nearly everyone in society."

"I hardly think they will be there. Though well-spoken enough, I surmised they were educated by tutors and seldom let off the leash, so to speak. They are definitely of age and might be in the market for a bride, but really, who would want to live in Blackwater Castle on the edge of the Serpent's Mouth and a great marshland?"

"We might." This time his sisters did speak simultaneously.

"I've been there," their father's deep voice claimed. "Met Blackwater only briefly, long enough to ascertain he would accept a gift of cannon from the crown to defend our coast from the French tyrant and not allow spies to infiltrate through his marshland. He's known as a recluse and the ministers felt he'd speak only with one with outranked him. Still, Blackwater offered no hospitality, and I spent the night at a small lodging in the village of Marston before returning to London. No sign of any sons while I was there, but then, he never allowed me within the castle proper as if I might make off with his silver. I doubt any of my daughters would want to stay there when they have Bellevue Hall and the townhouse at their disposal as long as they wish. No need to marry hastily."

The duchess considered for a moment. "However, we owe this family a debt. Perhaps James could write and invite them to stay at our townhouse for a visit as thanks for rescuing him. I will put them through their paces and see if they are in any way suitable for our daughters." She glanced out the windows where the rain had increased to pouring down like waterfalls against the glass. "We leave for London in two weeks if the weather clears and the roads are passable. You might put pen to paper this evening so as not to waste time, my dear son. I only wish I could keep *you* on the leash more often."

"I already pity those young men, but I will take care of the invitation."

"Terrible thing to say of your mother and your beautiful, spirited sisters! Let me make that up to you, my darling, and take that tenseness from your shoulders. You are so tired and harried with preparations for the removal to the city, and I am fatigued from my ride. Let's rest before the evening meal and leave our ungrateful children to their own devices. No more cake throwing, do you hear?" The duke helped his wife arise, and keeping possession of her dainty hand, made rapidly for their bedchamber.

"They are at it again," James said as he watched them rush toward the stairs.

"At what?" his innocent little sisters asked.

"Ask our mother before you marry the Hardacre boys. Now where can I find pen and paper?"

Two

In two weeks' time, the weather cleared and the roads hardened enough to begin the journey to London. The butler and some of the staff had gone ahead to open the townhouse while the duchess and her long entourage followed at a more leisurely pace. She shared the best carriage with her daughters and sometimes her husband and son if the circumstances of the journey became less clement, and they were forced from horseback. Maids, valets, and footmen followed in an older vehicle trailed by a baggage train bearing all the comforts the duchess felt necessary for the trek and survival in the city, including a supply of the wood she preferred to coal for the fireplaces.

Her route established over the years, they stopped for dinner at inns well-known to set a decent table and slept at others with a minimum of rats, lice, and bedbugs. Each evening, the maids shook out linens brought from Bellevue Hall and made up the beds outfitted with feather pillows. Each morning, they inspected the bedclothes for vermin before repacking them in the chests. With hampers filled with tidbits and bottles of beverages in case anyone hungered between meals, the small army made its way to London.

At the most recent stop, the duchess rubbed her temples and declared the constant chatter of her twin daughters had brought on a headache. After dining, her maid provided her with a tisane and soon after reentering the coach, she slept. Clio and Calliope watched for the telltale sign of their mother's regular breathing before beginning a whispered conversation.

"How our little sisters cried because they are not being brought along to London. Pandora thinks she is old enough at twelve, but she and Phemie both will be sent off to boarding school this autumn," Clio said with some satisfaction. "Frankly, I am glad we will not have to put up with their antics."

"That leaves only little Justinian in the nursery, but he is happy enough as long as he doesn't run out of books and mental challenges. I rather miss Joshua and Jason off at Eton, but we might see them while in the city,"

"Miss them? Miss toads and even a small snake put in our beds?"

"Well, we did capture all the little beasties and put them in Miss Thurgood's chamber—and off to boarding school we went. Good times," Callie sighed. Then, she asked what was really on her mind. "Do you think the Hardacre twins have answered James as yet?"

Clio shook her head. "Perhaps, but their letter will be at the townhouse. We must be patient. I know Mama set their visit to be mid-March so that we would have time to get established at Almack's and meet others before they arrive. She is not in favor of this idea, but will at least give it a try."

"I worry more about Papa. He thinks no one good enough for his daughters and will put them to the test. I do hope our twins are good with arms of all types and can deliver a mighty blow in the boxing ring if necessary. Of course, Danelagh met his approval, but then, doesn't Thalia always get her way? Papa nearly killed Iris' husband. I fear we might end up old maids."

"Callie, you worry far too much. Hasn't Mama always told us that with cleverness a woman might control her own fate, despite what men might think?"

"You believe we should elope then?"

"Only if absolutely necessary." Clio rummaged in the hamper even though they'd had a satisfactory repast with a rather salty haunch of ham not an hour ago at their last stop. She drew out a corked bottle, opened it, and sniffed. "Lemonade. Do you want to share?"

"Certainly, but isn't it always lemonade for ladies?" Callie took the first swig from the bottle and passed it back to her sister, both of them ignoring the cups in the basket. Their mother slept on, not aware enough to tell them to mind their manners. "I wish it were rum or at the very least, sherry."

"Rum rots the teeth, but enough sherry can make one tipsy. Remember when we stole Miss Stilton's decanter and shared it out amongst the girls? No one knew why our dormitory was so boisterous until they discovered the theft in the morning. I have to say the others did not squeal, but Miss Stilton suspected us even though she punished all with bread and water for several meals."

"As if a couple of days of starvation would deter a Longleigh woman. Clio, we are embarking on our own great adventure, I just know it. Mama, Thalia, and Iris have had theirs, and now we must have ours."

"I doubt if Papa will ever allow another of his daughters to leave England again because of their escapades," Clio sniffed. "Too bad for us!"

"I am sure there are adventures to be had in England, though we might have to seek them out. Are you ready?"

Clio raised her skirts and showed her sister the stiletto strapped to her right leg. "Papa has prepared us for anything, even when Mama objected."

Callie exposed her own weapon bound to her left leg. Both withdrew the knives and clashed them together. Their mother startled. Hastily, they returned the stilettos to the rather stylish sheaths the duchess has sewn for them in their signature colors of cherry and light blue, but their mama slept on.

"If Gareth and Tristan prove not to be gentlemen, we are prepared," Clio claimed.

"But, wouldn't it be wonderful if they weren't? We could defy them side by side or back to back with our knives in opposite hands as Papa taught us. They would be taken by surprise when we switch hands and show we can fight with either, thanks to Miss Thurgood forcing me to do my letters only with my right and you learning to use your left to keep her in confusion as to which of us was which."

"Ah, fond childhood memories, but I am so sorry about the number of times she rapped your fingers, poor Callie, and how often Mama switched your fork and spoon to the opposite hand and made you eat that way. I was so awfully clumsy when I first started to imitate you so no one could tell us apart."

"We succeeded very well. I doubt the Hardacres will be able to distinguish between us either."

The twin Longleigh daughters finished sharing the bottle of lemonade, giggling and carrying on so much in high spirits it might as well have been something stronger. Eventually, they did wake the duchess who asked both to pursue a book to preserve her sanity.

~ * ~

Gareth Hardacre, Viscount Marston, and his brother Tristan stood before their father in the great hall of the castle and waited while he perused the letter from Viscount Laughlin, their unexpected guest of some months ago.

"Go if you want, but do not expect me to attend with you. You'll discover nothing but pride and puffery in London. Gareth, find a bride and bring her back. Try to pick out a sturdy one and get your heir before she dies on you. The marshes take their toll on women. Tristan, if you come across a miss who will take a penniless second son, more power to you. Otherwise, wait here and see what the next ship to wreck brings ashore."

Lord Blackwater looked at the space between their broad shoulders unwilling to admit he couldn't tell his own sons one from the other when they were fully clothed. He ran his hands through his unbound, greasy grey hair and finally stared into each pair of dark blue eyes, their mother's eyes, bewitching eyes, he always said. All the rest of them belonged to him, from their lofty height and stalwart form to their long faces with hollows beneath the cheeks and obstinate jaws each marked with the slit of a cleft in the center.

They kept their chins clean-shaven but allowed for long, narrow side whiskers as dark a brown as their father's hair had once been.

"Laughlin mentions his twin sisters will be coming out into society this year. Perhaps we need look no farther than Bellevue House for brides," one of twins said.

"Not likely a duke's daughter will settle for a second son, unless she is extremely ugly or has a very poor dowry. Tristan, you'll have to seize one from the rocks as I did. Keep her captive and put a child in her belly so she'll beg for marriage, as I did with your mother. Had I known my older brother would drown, I could have followed a more traditional course. Ah well, that's water out to sea again."

Tristan looked at Gareth or vice versa. "Do you think they will be ugly or maybe brawny like their brother, and that is why we have been invited?"

"Good for you if they are! What matters are hips like a brood mare and tits of good size made for mothering, even if they insist on a wet nurse." Their father shared his wisdom on choosing a bride.

One son said rather wistfully, "Mama was beautiful. I remember that much."

"That she was and dead of marsh fever after only six years in Blackwater. She ensorcelled me with those deep-sea blue eyes of hers soon as I plucked her from the waves. I saved her life and she owed me her honor, but she wasn't the choice I should have made. Be careful. The ladies of London are wily and always on the lookout for a fine title and the lands and wealth that go with it."

"Then, we go with your blessing?"

'Yes, go, and take Oskar with you to be your manservant."

Both young men considered the minion who stood at their father's right shoulder. "But, Father, a person of his size with a shaven head and only one eye might be mistaken for a ruffian in the city," one of them objected.

Oskar smoothed his scalp. "Keeps the lice down, ye know."

"He lost that eye serving at the Battle of the Nile under Lord Nelson. Tell their high and mighties that! Put him in some fancy livery and no one will object to his presence. He's done well enough for me and will do the same for my sons."

"Oskar, you might have to abandon the gold earring," a son suggested.

"Guess I could." Oscar shrugged his brutish shoulders. "Ain't been to London in many a year. Who knows what they wear there now?"

Lord Blackwater rose from his carved chair and moved to one of the great chests lining the stone wall. He withdrew a large key hanging from a thong under his loose shirt worn without waistcoat or jacket and turned it the lock. He threw each of his sons a hefty pouch that clinked when they caught them. "For expenses. Go pack your trunks."

"But our invitation is not until mid-March. I expect they want to get settled in their townhouse before then."

"This is a battle for a bride, my sons, and don't think it ain't. In any battle, surprise is an advantage. I learned that from the great Lord Nelson. Meet them at the door when their carriage arrives and see how they deal with the situation. Learn all you can about this Laughlin's family and make your decision a wise one. Now get out of my sight until you leave."

~ * ~

As they were no more fond of being in their father's presence than he was of having them around, the twins left immediately for their shared chamber in the tower. Once the heavy door closed behind then, they spilled the contents of the pouches on their beds. Blackwater had given them a pirate's treasure in gold coins, Spanish and French and some British as well, a generous offering from a man who scrimped on everything out of sheer stinginess.

"Not a very warm sendoff, but at least he didn't lock us in the dungeon to prevent our going." Tristan began to count his coins.

"That could still happen if we irritate him in any way, you know."

"Now that we are men and he is weakening, the servants wouldn't allow it. They'd want to curry favor with the upcoming marquess, Gary, and would release us if we couldn't escape ourselves. We did get fairly good at it."

"As he intended, I believe, to strengthen us. I'd like to think he did not do it out of cruelty, Tris." Gareth, heir to the entirety of the castle and its lands, simply shoved his largesse back into its sack. "Pack lightly. We have only workaday clothes, and you saw how Laughlin was dressed. He looked elegant even wading ashore from a beached ship."

"Yes, our first outing in London must be to the tailor's shop. Until then, we wear our Sunday best and hope it isn't too outmoded. If we ape the viscount, we should do well enough with our manners. If nothing else, the old man made us resourceful."

"Hard lessons learned. London cannot be half as bad as Blackwater. Promise me you won't reveal that I am the heir, Tris. I cannot abide the fawning when people figure it out."

"As I enjoy a little fawning, not having much of it, certainly we will play the twin game for all it is worth. I am more than ready for London."

With that, Tristan began stuffing a trunk since neither had ever been given access to a valet other than Oskar who had never packed other than a seaman's kit. The greater question might be, "Was London ready for them?"

Three

The ducal coach drew up before Bellevue House where two tradesmen and a brute who might have been a butcher or a one-eyed blacksmith lounged on the small flight of marble steps leading to the front door. One slouched in profile against a carved lion and the other stared at the coach while the muscular bald man had the temerity to squat on the landing. Two small, battered trunks cluttered the walkway.

The duchess frowned at them as her footman scurried to open the carriage door and put down the steps. "Already a plague of merchants wanting our trade. I cannot figure why Busby hasn't sent them around back to speak to the housekeeper."

The one who had only presented a profile to their view turned. The girls shrieked, "Our twins!" loud enough to be heard and received a glare from their mother.

James drilled fingers into his ears to close out their shrill voices. He'd ridden in the coach to keep the dust from his clothes for the entry into London, but had enough of their chatter. "Yes, they are. Mama, allow me to go first before Papa catches up and throws them into the road for being impertinent."

"Proceed, then," the duchess acceded and watched with interest.

James stooped his lengthy form to leave the vehicle, reset his tall hat, and came forth to greet their guests. "Gareth and Tristan Hardacre, here you are at Bellevue House, early but not unwelcome."

"We thought to make the most of the Season by arriving on its cusp," one said boldly.

"Our journey proved shorter than we calculated, fine weather, good roads," the other brother answered mildly. The uncouth, bald creature snorted, drawing attention to himself. "Our man, Oskar. Stand up, Oskar. Allow the gentlewomen to pass."

"Ah, Mama, allow me to introduce Gareth, Viscount Marston and his brother, Lord Tristan Hardacre. Have I got that right?" Both young men nodded. "My mother, Lady Flora, Duchess of Bellevue and my sisters, Lady Clio and Lady Calliope Longleigh."

The girls, clustered one on each side of their mother, stared speechless, their mouths half open in delight at the sight of two such comely if poorly dressed young men. Finally, Clio managed to say, "So very pleased to meet you."

"Very pleased," Callie echoed as both bobbed a shallow curtsy.

"Oh, no, the pleasure is all ours."

The duchess offered her hand, and one of them bent over it rather quickly, passing it on to his brother. Lady Flora beckoned a footman. "Summon Busby at once to see to our guests." It took only a single rap of the large, brass knocker to bring the butler to their service.

"Busby, I do not want Viscount Marston and his brother to be left standing on the curb a moment longer."

With the tips of his ears reddening, Busby immediately tasked the footmen to bring the men's traveling boxes inside at once and carry them up to the guest suites. "I beg your pardon, Lady Flora, I had no knowledge visitors were expected so soon." The butler did not mention that the pair hardly looked liked gentlemen likely to be entertained at Bellevue House, given their attire and poorly barbered hair.

"I tried to show him the bloody invite, but the bugger slammed the door in me face." Oskar growled like a provoked watchdog.

"And show this—this manservant to his quarters at well," Busby said, drawing himself to full lofty height and peering down his very long nose at twins' valet as if he were a cur in need of discipline.

Before the group on the stairs could enter, the duke arrived on his gray steed, a horse large enough to bear a knight in full armor and so a good fit for a man his size. He swung easily out of the saddle and sized up his unexpected guests immediately.

"Early are you? I like young men who show some initiative." He moved to clap both on the back with a welcoming blow of his large hands that showed his strength. Both stood steady under the onslaught.

"This, needless to say, is my husband, Pearce Longleigh, Duke of Bellevue," Lady Flora said with exasperation. "Could we possibly all come in off the street?"

The men stood aside to allow the ladies to enter. "Handsome," murmured Clio to Callie as their mother passed. "Not cows," one of their guests uttered quietly to his brother.

"Promising," thought the duchess.

~ * ~

All had agreed to repair to their chambers to wash off the dirt of travel, rest and change clothes before meeting in the drawing room before supper. Clio and Callie stripped to their undergarments and sponged themselves with warm water bought in a basin but did not sleep. Instead they stretched out on the featherbed they were to share and talked of the Hardacre brothers.

"I think James did not do their masculine attributes justice. They are certainly tall and well-made. The cleft in their manly chins only makes their faces more handsome."

"Blue eyes deep enough to drown in and such nice side whiskers. I never like them when they are too full, but these frame their faces perfectly."

"Which do you think is the heir?" Clio fluffed the pillow under her head and gazed at the canopy over the bed so charmingly decorated with embroidered wildflowers, their mother's needlework.

"No telling. They are playing the same game we always did to others, I'd bet. Smart of them to want to be admired for one's self instead of for a title."

"Then how shall we figure out whom to marry? I am first born and should have the heir."

"No one would know that if the midwife hadn't tied a red ribbon to your wrist directly after birth and put a blue upon mine. Not that it matters much with daughters. We should accept the one that pleases us most and go live at Castle Blackwater together. It's as simple as that." Callie played with one of her black curls, twining it around her finger, the habit her mother so disliked.

"Not simple! What if we both prefer the same twin?"

"A double dilemma. Then I suppose one of us marries and the other does not. I can always stay by your side as a maiden aunt to your children."

"You would do that for me, Callie?"

"If we could stay close, Clio, I would."

"Well, I think you are too pretty and spritely to remain unmarried for long."

"A trifle vain of you since we appear exactly alike. When I passed the Hardacres, one of them said, 'Not cows.' What do you think that meant?"

Clio laughed. "I believe they thought James invited them here to pawn off his two homely sisters. I gather they were pleased at our appearance and expressed that rather crudely. As for theirs, James will hone off the rough edges in no time."

~ * ~

"Not cows nor mares. I've never seen such pert little figures or quite so many bouncing black curls beneath a bonnet," Tristan said as he settled comfortably into a deep leather chair before the fireplace in the bedchamber he'd been assigned.

A dressing room separated his quarters from his brother's, an arrangement probably intended to accommodate married couples but very convenient for them as well. Oskar snored on a cot in this middle space amid washing necessities, a dressing table for the arrangement of hair, a full-length mirror, and other paraphernalia required by the ton for bathing and getting into clothes. He needed nothing more than a blanket to be comfortable in the small area.

"But eyes like marsh deer, so large, brown and bright." Gareth in a matching chair put his feet up on a hassock next to his brother's stockinged toes.

"They are brown as does, too. Do you think that is why Viscount Laughlin invited the likes of us here, to find men who might not require their wives to be lily white of complexion?"

"They are the daughters of a very wealthy duke. Unless their dowries are niggardly, they will have no trouble finding a match, not with those pretty little faces. I fear they might expire in childbirth or give way to ill health at Blackwater." Gareth expressed his concern.

"Their mother has birthed at least three, and she appears to be as delicate as a porcelain shepherdess. Looks can be deceiving, as we well know," Tristan asserted.

"I would feel guilty if one of them died having my heir," Gareth countered.

"*You* would. You never wanted to slit the throat of any deer our hounds brought down unless our father made you. I'd be grateful if I got to keep the dowry. We need to learn more about the Longleighs tonight. Let's roust Oskar from his rest and set him to brushing our clothes and shining our boots. Isn't that what a valet does?"

"I'm guessing so." The heir of Blackwater went to shake their man awake.

Four

The Hardacres made a better impression at supper than upon arrival. They appeared in the drawing room dressed in blue broadcloth that flattered their eyes. They'd scraped their chins clean of travel stubble, and their shoes gleamed as smartly as an admiral's boots. If their hair still reached their shoulders, it was clean and well-brushed if not properly arranged. Their neckcloths were snowy, the knots tying them very plain unlike James Longleigh's which excelled in complexity. All of this impressed the duchess favorably as she observed their every move.

They did not swill the hot soup but waited for others to dip their spoons first. Since the dinner was informal this first night in London, they passed the cold dishes around without spilling and politely remembered please and thank you when requesting mustard or horseradish to enhance the meats. Perhaps their conversation lacked wit, but it was not unpleasant.

"Tell us, are there anymore Longleighs? Have you brothers and sisters? We are all Lord Blackwater has to offer," the more talkative one asked.

His question generated laughter around the table. "A great many more," the duchess answered. "We have a scandalous number of children, ten to be exact."

"All living?" the quiet one said, quite awed.

"Oh my, yes. We are a hardy breed. You have met James, our eldest. Then we have two married daughters, Thalia, Countess of Danelagh, and Iris, wife to Viscount Valls, our twins here, Joshua and Jason at Eton, and Pandora, Euphemia, and Justinian still in the nursery. The world will never lack for Longleighs."

"Gives you a certain amount of freedom knowing your father has so many spare sons," James said as he speared a slice of smoked venison conveyed all the way from Bellevue Hall and placed it on his dish.

"I do wish you wouldn't speak as if you were replaceable," his mother chided.

"But I am, Mama, so I am in no haste to marry. I promised you a Season at home and here I am, keeping my word, but do not push every eligible girl at Almack's in my face if you do force me to go there. I fancy a trip to Egypt this winter now that Napoleon is out of the way, and I don't plan to be tied down by an engagement."

The duchess sighed wearily. "Almack's is always short of men to dance with the young ladies. I expect you to do your part while you are here. Gentlemen, do you enjoy dancing?" She turned the conversation deftly from her roving son to her guests.

"Our father was chary with money for anything he considered fripperies. Dance masters fell into that category," one of them answered.

The other said, "We did learn some country dances in Marston. The girls in the village were eager to teach us the steps among other things." The Hardacre twins exchanged grins, though one of them quickly stated, "They did not complain over much about our treading of their feet, but I suppose those dances aren't done at this Almack's."

"Indeed they are," the duchess replied. "The patronesses feel reels preferable for propriety."

"Shawnee courtship dances put them all to shame," the duke added. His wife blushed ever so slightly.

"I'd like to hear about them," one Hardacre said.

"Not polite dinner conversation, I am afraid," James informed him, saving his mother from further embarrassment.

"Do you know the cotillion? There are sure to be several of those," the duchess asked, putting the conversation back where it belonged.

Two shaggy heads shook a "no."

"But, Mama, we can teach them tonight if you will play the piano for us," Clio piped up. "You would like to learn, wouldn't you, Viscount Marston?"

"Yes," both of their guests replied at once. Their audience laughed politely.

"Ah, I know this game, a favorite of twins. Keep your secret for a while. You will have no trouble telling our girls apart. From birth, Clio always had a bit of red on her person...tonight the red silk roses in her hair. Calliope will wear something blue like the cornflowers on her muslin. Woe to the nursery maid who did not follow my rule. However, I've since discovered other ways of telling them apart. I am sure your father has his ways as well." The duchess cocked her head, encouraging the young men to speak.

The genial, white-toothed smiles of their guests disappeared. "That he does."

"But none so charming as yours," the more soft-spoken one added.

Pudding, dried fruits, fresh oranges from the conservatory at Bellevue Hall, nuts and cheeses, both sharp and mild, covered the table as the servants cleared the main dishes. The ladies soon withdrew, leaving the Hardacres at the mercy of the duke. "Over to you," the duchess whispered to her mate as she led the girls away.

He told them all about Shawnee courting dances over the port. "Shocked my daughter's governess so terribly when she came across the duchess and myself celebrating our anniversary as we did among the red Indians that the woman fainted, then resigned. I find the English to be excessively proper."

He opened a drawer in the sideboard, turned his back and used the pisspot hidden inside. Washing his hands in a basin of scented water, he asked, "Anyone else? No, then," and continued the conversation. "My Shawnee blood gives strength to my sons and makes my daughters brown and beautiful, don't you think."

"Absolutely." The pair could not agree fast enough.

As his guests relaxed, the duke followed up with an assessment of their skill at manly arts. "Saber or epee?" he asked.

"Saber and cutlass. Our father was once a navy man and would not allow our tutelage in anything else."

"My newest son-in-law favors the epee, an effete weapon, it seems to me."

"Both can kill you," James remarked casually, though his words seemed to have deeper meaning.

His father ignored that. "You ride, of course?'

"All the way here, but we've never hunted foxes on horseback. The marshes really don't allow for that."

"We might arrange a fox hunt sometime in the future. We must keep the estate clear of vermin. Have you trained with pistols and rifles?"

"Excessively," one of young men replied drolly. "Not much else to do at Castle Blackwater."

"How about pugilism?" The duke cracked two walnuts in his fist as was his wont and offered them to his guests, but that, too, might have had a deeper meaning.

"No proper training in the boxing ring, but we've brawled often enough, wrestled, too."

"I must take you to Gentleman Jackson's for a go at it. He will refine your style and then, we might spar with each other. You are somewhat heavier than James, but I warn you, he is quick on his feet and strikes like a viper."

The twins grinned. "We'd be pleased to take him on, one at a time of course." James grinned back at them even more wolfishly.

"Time enough for that. I fear tomorrow you will have to see a good tailor and a barber. My wife will assuredly drag us all to insufferable

Almack's for the girls' first presentation and you must spruce up for the occasion. James will see to you."

James took the chance to tweak his father. "Are you sure you won't come and have that mane of yours chopped off and your hair put in better order? You might consider getting pantaloons and a more stylish jacket as well." He eyed father's knee breeches and lacy cuffs.

"Being a duke has many advantages, one of them being I can dress as I please and be as eccentric as I like. People will still kiss my arse. Besides, your mother would swoon if I ever cut my hair. She likes to run her fingers through its length." That shut the boy up properly or maybe improperly.

"I believe the ladies have waited long enough." The Duke of Bellevue led the way to the drawing room.

~ * ~

In no time at all, the servants carried away the tea and coffees services and rolled up a Turkey carpet to clear the floor for dancing. The duchess took her place at the pianoforte, placed her fingers lightly on the keys and prepared to assess the skills and personalities of the Hardacre twins even more.

"Do keep in mind that I cannot match any of my daughters in their skill at the keyboard," she said modestly. "My hands are simply too small."

"Nonsense! They get their talent in singing and playing entirely from you, my dear," the duke insisted.

"Ah, but there is that Italian opera singer in the Longleigh ancestry. Thalia must have inherited her magnificent voice."

"Your voice is as fine as hers. How I remember you singing in the wilderness, my petite yellow canary." The duke squeezed his wife's small shoulders affectionately. His children shuddered, but their guests smiled broadly.

"Please play something at once," James begged.

His sisters quickly beckoned to their male counterparts to stand at their sides. The Hardacre boys towered over the girls much as did the duke over the duchess. Clio and Callie gazed at them sidelong through lowered lashes, their black curls trembling, like the shy and proper maidens they were not—as James and his parents both knew.

"We should teach them the cotillion, but that requires four couples. Come Papa and James. Pretend to be dancing with a lady so we might show them the steps," Callie begged.

"Always glad to oblige my daughters." The duke arose and took his place.

"Always happy to show off your calves, my dear, and they are magnificent," his wife remarked. "Get into position, James. Don't be a stick-in-the-mud. You know you dance very nicely."

James joined the group, and the duchess began playing rather slowly for the sake of those new to the figures. Clio called the first of the changes. "Take hands, balance, and rigadoon."

The Hardacre boys stopped right there as both the duke and James began a complicated series of hops and leg flinging too difficult to be easily copied. The duke performed vigorously, James more gracefully.

"Perhaps you should start with a simple beaten step. Hop four times on one foot and extend your other leg at the side. Bring it back to your side at the calf as the Highlanders do," Callie suggested gently. The young men managed this decently enough.

"Now, chasse', that's a glide, right eight steps, then left eight steps. Very good!" Clio encouraged. "Right hand together, balance and rigadoon with your partner, now with the left hand."

The rest went a bit easier on the novices with a wheel formed by the ladies in the center of the square and then by the men. After several turns through the song, they managed a Grand Chain and then back to the beginning again, over and over until the Hardacres got a feel for it. At last, the duchess declared her fingers might fall off if she continued to pound the keys any longer and put an end to the lesson. She called for cheese and crackers and a nightcap to help them all sleep soundly after their exertions and shooed them off to their bedchambers soon afterwards.

~ * ~

Clio and Callie lay side by side in their bed, the only light coming from a few fireplace embers glowing through a coat of ashes. "What do you think of them now?" Clio whispered.

"Unpolished, certainly, but we can bring out their shine. They dance more like Papa without the skill than James. Perhaps that will keep other young ladies away."

"I think not, since one of them has a title. But which one?" Clio pondered. "Which one?"

~ * ~

A similar conversation took place in the guestrooms where Gareth and Tristan sat up together allowing their blood to cool before trying to rest. "I think we did very well with the dinner and got along famously with the duke," Gareth said.

"Well enough, but the old man will make us prove ourselves before he gives up his daughters. We acted like blasted fools in the dancing. Chasse', rigadoon, who knew what that meant?" Tristan picked up a poker and provoked the fire into a shower of sparks."

"We only want practice. Don't be so gloomy."

"A second son comes into the world with no prospects. That incites gloom. I suspect a wealthy widow or a girl with twenty-thousand will expect her suitor to dance well, not just hop about and hope for the best."

"Well, you are at no disadvantage yet, since no one knows which of us is which."

"They will if we take off our shirts," Tristan continued pessimistically.

"I doubt well-bred young ladies will tear off your clothing, Tris. At the gymnasium, we will simply keep our shirts on."

"I don't know about *these* well-bred young ladies. They give me a certain feeling."

"In your loins? I felt it, too, just looking at them doing all that bobbing from the view above their pretty bosoms. Brown they might be, but very bouncy." Gareth drew a smile from his brother at last.

"That, too, but I believe there is more to them than meets the eye. Speaking of which, I am ready to close mine."

Five

The next day, the Hardacre boys had their blue eyes opened to the wider world. Rousted out of their beds by James, they stepped into the ducal carriage at ten a.m. before the ladies made an appearance at breakfast. The duke had no intention of being dragged to a tailor or a barber. His valet did for him, and his tailor had his measurements on file. Both despaired of ever bringing the man into the nineteenth century in style. He asked to be let down at 13 Bond Street, the location of Gentleman's Jackson Saloon, for some vigorous exercise and promised to meet them at his club for luncheon. No sense in going home as the ladies would most likely be out dropping calling cards like snow settling on silver trays.

In the care of James, the Hardacres were barbered within an inch of their flesh except for a stylish mop on top and having a few modish curls formed by an iron they thought only women used, James remarked he envied their closely cut side whiskers. "They do make a fine frame for a face. Thanks to my Shawnee heritage, all my attempts at them have been rather skimpy, so I do without."

On to the tailor claiming to be an exile from the French court, where both of the twins were measured, prodded, and touched in places they would rather have left alone to get the proper tight fit of their pantaloons, jackets, waistcoats, and oh yes, knee breeches for dancing at Almack's. At the end of the process, Gareth held out a few of the gold coins to the fawning little man with the tape around his neck. "Will this be enough?"

The tailor's mouth dropped open. He licked away his spittle as his hand reached for the money. James slapped the fingers away. "Send the reckoning to my address at the end of the month as you do for every gentleman."

So close, so close to immediate payment, the tailor's dark eyes seemed to say. Gareth did not make the same mistake at the cobbler's shop when the Italian knelt at their feet and fitted them for magnificent new boots and dancing shoes, or at the haberdashery where fine linen shirts, neckcloths, stockings, a pair of tall hats, and gloves to cover their somewhat coarse hands were purchased. The carriage hauled their boxes and packages to Bellevue House, leaving them free to dine at the club at their leisure.

"I've done my exercise for the day, but if you are tired of shopping, I would be pleased to introduce you to Gentleman Jackson himself after we dine," the duke suggested as he carved a fat capon for his party.

"I never imagined the purchase of clothing could be so fatiguing," one twin remarked.

"My wife and daughters claim that it is. What, no energy left for the gymnasium?" His voice offered a small challenge. The duke helped himself to small potatoes swimming in butter and parsley and carrots nicely glazed.

"Frankly, I would relish some exertion after all that shearing and primping and shoeing like some prize animal," the one who tended to speak first and more firmly, the heir perhaps, answered.

James set them straight. "That's exactly what you are to the ladies of the ton, at least the one with a title," he answered as he broke off a piece of bread and buttered it. "Whenever I enter a room during the Season, I feel as if I might end up being led away by the halter with a young miss and her mother hanging on either side. I am very much enjoying your little ruse. Makes me wish I had a twin to play such a game with them."

"As a twin, you are never alone and always have a friend, another benefit." One twin at least enjoyed his repast immensely as he picked up the leg of the chicken and ate it from the bone. No problem with dinnerware and multiple dishes when dining among men.

"But quite a lot of confusion. I know our girls deceive us at times. Mainly, I stick to the color devise and assume the one with the cherry trim is Clio, but I suspect they are adept at changing roles. My father had a shameful penchant for acting upon the stage—in disguise of course. Most of my children seem to have inherited his talent, so watch out for them." The duke appropriated the other chicken leg as no one else seemed to want it.

"Papa failed to mention he is adept at imitating almost any beast of the forest. Frequently scared us shitless when we spent the night in the Indian lodge at Bellevue Hall. First, he'd fill our heads with tales of bears and wolves, then send us to our pallets. After a while, we'd hear prowling beasts grunting and panting nearby. Papa of course, who can move very quietly for a big man."

"I always found you huddled in a clutch, weapons extended, when I entered covered in the bear pelt. A Longleigh never goes down without a fight. Then I'd wrestle with them all in good fun, though I nearly lost my fingers to Pandora when I reached a paw through a break in the bark to tickle her, and she attacked me with a tomahawk. Just grabbed that little wrist in time to save my hand." The duke grinned with pride over his fierce family.

"You might as well know my sisters are little vixens," James said. "Beware!"

"They are spirited, simply spirited, James."

"Oh, we like spirited," one of his guests assured him.

"Our father also played games with us, not quite so charming, but he did make men of us." This twin seemed to have lost his appetite. He set down his knife and fork and took a long draft of his wine.

"Exactly what I want for my daughters, real men, not these dandies who mince about the dance floor and worry more about their striped pantaloons than their partners."

"Then, a toast to no striped pantaloons," one of the twins offered, raising his glass merrily. They could all drink to that.

~ * ~

The ladies returned home replete with gossip and enough refreshments to render an afternoon meal unnecessary. They settled in the drawing room by a brisk fire taking the damp and chill from the March air and asked only for hot tea to restore them. The gentlemen joined them late in the day. Two pairs of dark brown eyes widened as the refurbished male twins entered, followed by James who had acquired a bruise on one high cheekbone.

His mother fussed. "Accident or brawling this time, James?"

"Neither really. I sparred with our guests at Gentlemen Jackson's and one of them clipped me fairly hard."

"My apologies. After your jab to my gut, I reacted too strongly. I sort of forgot we were having a friendly bout." Shamefaced, a Hardacre accepted a cup of tea doctored heavily with sugar and cream much like the cup the duchess handed to her husband.

She offered the same to James. "Come, this will pick you up after your exertions."

"I'd rather a brandy. No hard feelings, but my cheek does throb."

"Yes, he landed quite a blow," the duke recounted enthusiastically. "They don't keep their guards up well, so James got the belly punch in, but the retaliation was instant and hard. Knocked poor James on his bum. Not bad for men so modest they fight in their shirts."

"Really?" said Clio, delighted. "Which one of you did it?" A twin raised a hand. "Did he bruise your stomach as well?"

"No, ah, Lady—." He quickly checked her person and found cherry red ribbons gathering a cluster of black curls on either side of her face. "Lady Clio. I hardened my muscles, you see."

"I'd like to see."

"Clio! No more talk of seeing men's muscles or descriptions of pugilism in the drawing room. Let the men discuss that after our supper. And not a word of such things when we go to Almack's next evening. James, are our guests properly outfitted to attend with us?" the duchess questioned.

"I asked for some haste on their dancing slippers and formal garments. Luigi and Monsieur Labit have never failed me."

"Very well. Go change for dinner, my dears." She shooed her girls from the room when obviously they would have preferred to stay staring at the Hardacre twins sporting their new coiffures.

~ * ~

"I do find them much handsomer with their hair shorn," Clio declared as the maid she shared with her sister lowered a gown of palest pink over her head, pulled tight the ribbons across the back, and fluffed the puffs at the top of the sleeves.

The aptly named maid, Finch, small and possessing enough energetic movement to provide service for two young ladies, fluttered to Callie's side to provide the same assistance, only this time lowering a dress of lightest blue. As Callie's head reemerged, she said, "I don't know. I liked their hair longer. It reminded me of Papa a little. But, I adore their side whiskers, so masculine."

"I wish we could have seen if one of them had a bruised belly. Then we'd be able to tell them apart for a time."

"Wouldn't do any good as we still don't know which is the viscount."

"Well, I am glad one of them put James in his place—or on his bum. I've always wanted to be tall enough to do the same when he lords it over us. Probably only Thalia could manage it because of her height, but she is far too lady-like."

The girls sat side by side on a bench at their dressing table waiting for Finch to put the finishing touches on their own coiffures. The maid tucked in escaped strands with pins and added small clusters of silk apple blossoms and blue violets to the bunches of ribbons holding their curls in place. She offered them drops of single pearls for their ear lobes and fastened a strand of the same about each of their necks, gifts from their father for their debut.

"I think you are throwing these pearls before swine if the gentlemen are anything like their manservant. I've never seen a greater lout with all his belching and scratching in unseemly places. I do hope he hasn't brought lice into the house," Finch stated. "I'd save the pearls for Almack's. They stand out so well against your darker complexion."

"They can be worn both tonight and at Almack's, Finch, and everyone that scratches an itch is not louse-ridden," Callie rebuked her.

"I'd bet this mangy dog is, though not upon his shaven head. There you go, all ready to sup and dazzle the young men if you really wish to. Remember as daughters of the Duke of Bellevue, you have wider choices than most. You look so lovely, so grown. Not my curly-headed infants anymore." Finch dabbed her eyes with a hankie from her sleeve. She'd worked her way up from nursery maid, and past thirty and her prime, had little prospect of having her own babes. "I'll be right here to help you prepare for your slumbers, but please do knock as I plan to keep the door locked as long as that—that—crude person prowls the halls."

"I believe his name is Oskar, and he lost his eye serving Lord Nelson, I was told. Please give him some courtesy," Callie directed as she rose to leave for dinner.

Leaving Finch hovering in the doorway, the girls proceeded side by side down the stairs. Clio whispered in her sister's ear, "Like having two mothers with Finch fussing over us and giving advice."

"I think that is why Mama chose her," Callie agreed. "Another pair of eyes on all our doings."

Six

The duchess urged her daughters to sleep as late as possible on Wednesday morning so that they might be fresh for their introduction at Almack's Assembly Rooms, but numerous deliveries, even though brought around the back, woke them. Most of the packages were addressed to the Hardacres. All the seamstresses around Bellevue Hall had worked their nimble fingers night and day to complete suitable wardrobes for the girls before they left home once the duchess decided they'd had enough schooling. Or perhaps she felt she couldn't get them into yet another female academy. However, Bellevue's daughters would certainly add to their fripperies in London. In fact, their mother took them out to shop for plumes directly after breakfast to calm their nerves and keep them out of the way of their guests whom James tutored in matters of dress.

He recommended dark stockings to wear with the snug black knee breeches and long-tailed jackets. "Papa will appear in white silk hose with clocks along the legs. He does like to show off his calves, but this will be far more striking for the two of you, a nice contrast to your white waistcoats and neckcloths. I will show your man how to tie some of the less difficult but still stylish knots if he can manage."

They beckoned to Oskar lurking in a dim corner of the bedchamber. He came forth reluctantly knitting his big hands and thick fingers together repeatedly. "Course I can manage. If I can tie any number of seaman's knots, a piece of linen ain't going to confound me."

James raised his dark brows, but was forced to lower them when Oskar proved strangely adept. "Job well done, my good man."

"And for your reward, may we present your new livery." One of his charges held out a bulky package. "Go into the dressing room and try it on."

The twins snickered as they waited, making James all the more curious. Finally, Oskar emerged clad in green satin with orange ruching on the sides of the knee britches and running in stripes up the jacket. His legs, like tree trunks enclosed in white silk, ended in sturdy buckled shoes highly polished.

"I look like a bleedin' Amazonian parrot, for Christ's sake."

Obviously holding in their laughter, one of the young men held forth a box. "But you haven't seen the full effect yet." He withdrew a powdered wig with a triple row of side curls and a short tail already tied with a black bow. Settling it on the bald man's head, the twin said, "There you go, and you have a fine tricorn hat to go atop it. Now, aren't you a sight?"

"A sight bound to draw mockery—though I'll admit the shoes are the best I've ever had on me feet."

"Oh, the tailor assured us a footman cannot be too gaudy or too tall. The point is to draw attention, I presume, and you certainly do that. We guessed your size well, simply kept saying larger as he brought out his samples," the other brother said. A small hiccup of a laugh escaped his lips.

"I ain't givin' up me gold earring." Oskar's brutish lips pushed out as he fingered one fat, pierced lobe.

"No need, my good man. You will stand out even more with that adornment," James answered. "That's what it is all about amongst the ton, standing out. Do have him ride on the back of the carriage tonight. He'll be the talk of Almack's: a one-eyed, earring-wearing footman in orange and green and none too pretty."

"Is London society as bad as all that?" one of the twins asked.

"Oh, worse, far, far worse as you shall see," James assured them.

~ * ~

Thanks to the small stature of the duchess and her daughters, all seven of them were able to cram into the carriage with the duke, a Hardacre on either side, sitting across from the already bored James and the females quivering with excitement for the festivities to begin. The girls did look fetching in their identical gauzy white gowns, each one bearing a curling plume affixed to her black curls with a jeweled clip, small rubies in one, tiny sapphires in the other, both surrounded by seed pearls. Their eardrops shook with their nerves and a light but flattering dew gathered on their bosoms beneath the strands of pearls. "My little beauties," their father proclaimed them.

"All is well," the duchess assured her daughters. "I procured tickets for our guests, though few have heard of Lord Blackwater. Titled and eligible men are more likely to be welcomed than some others."

"Ten guineas a head for bread and butter, dry cake, and weak ratafia," the duke grumbled.

"That is why we had our supper before coming. I wouldn't want the girls—or yourself— to faint from hunger." Lady Flora snapped her fan open in a way that said she would brook no more complaining from anyone tonight. The breeze she created cooled her overheated daughters somewhat.

"We'd be glad to reimburse you the expense," a Hardacre twin said and reached into his waistcoat.

"Stop doing that or someone will knock you over the head for your purse," James advised.

"Not with Oskar riding with us. He may look the fool in that costume, but he is a mighty brawler, handy with a knife, too."

"Good to know. A man should never go unarmed, even to affairs such as this," the duke added, thumping his sword cane on the floor of the carriage.

"You will not threaten anyone this evening, Pearce. Allow the girls the pleasure of dancing with many gentlemen, not only the ones you approve." She closed her fan and rapped her husband lightly across the knuckles.

"I suppose. Here we are, like it or not."

Handed down before the disappointingly plain building that was Almack's on King Street, the girls walked demurely behind their parents and before the other gentlemen. The interior might also have been a letdown to some, but not to young ladies just coming out into society. Dark eyes shining, they had never seen a ballroom so huge. Enormous mirrors reflected the light of double-tiered chandeliers. Gilded columns and decorative medallions ornamented the walls. Velvet ropes surrounded the dancing floor and partitioned off other spaces, keeping the area clear, and an impressively-sized orchestra tuned their instruments at one end of the space. Remaining unimpressed, James covered a yawn with his gloved hand.

"Rather like the livestock market in Marston with the ropes and all the people milling about," a Hardacre twin remarked to James as they queued forward to be introduced to the Lady Patronesses of the place.

"That's it exactly. Soon the fillies and mares will be trotted out for all to see and judged on their deportment, their beauty, their breeding, and most of all, their dowries. It's a marriage mart," James informed them.

Overhearing, the duchess contradicted. "Some say Almack's is the seventh heaven of the fashionable world," she sniffed.

"Certainly I've never seen so many prime fillies in one place. It might well be heaven to me," a Hardacre answered.

"Be careful to show no favoritism, not even to my sisters, or you will be leg-shackled before the night is out," James warned.

"You seem to have managed to escape," the other said.

"Generally, I stay out of the country during the Season, but the twins can be difficult. I promised my mother I would help with them. Regretting it already."

One of the patronesses spied him and stretched her somewhat stringy neck to get a better look around the bulk of the duke. She beckoned him forward. "Viscount Laughlin, so delighted to have you with us this evening. And who are your friends?"

"Here we go," he muttered and made his bow. "Allow me to introduce the sons of the Marquess of Blackwater, Gareth, Viscount Marston, and his brother, Lord Tristan Hardacre." Both of the young men bowed at exactly the same time.

"Ha! How alike you are. Now which is which? Who is Viscount Marston?" the patroness inquired as she cocked her head crowned with three black plumes like an exotic bird come to roost in London.

The Hardacre boys poked a finger at each other. "He is."

"Ah, I see, a jest. Then allow me to ask where your country seat is located. I do not recall a Marquess of Blackwater." She pondered with her fan tapping lightly against her faintly rouged lips.

One of the young men spoke up. "Our father rarely leaves the castle which is on the Kentish coast overlooking the marshes. We derive our income mostly from sheep."

"You see," said the other. "He was born a second son and married before coming into the title. He saw no need to come to London to seek a bride."

The patroness's dark, bird-like eyes grew brighter at the mention of brides, sheep, and a castle. "Do allow me to introduce my niece to you before the dancing begins."

"Ahem," the duchess interrupted. "We are here tonight to bring our daughters into society. My twins, Lady Clio and Lady Calliope Longleigh." Her girls made their curtsies, bobbing up again as if on springs, a little too quickly, and setting their thick black curls into motion.

"*Comme charmart*! Like two *colorful* china dolls from the same maker," the patroness exclaimed, though she obviously eyed them as rivals to her niece and sought out any flaws from their topknots to their toes and settled on their brown complexions.

"I assure you God and my husband made them," the duchess said.

"More likely the devil," James mumbled. His mother gave him a swift elbow jab that seemed almost accidental as if he'd simply gotten in her way.

"Point out your niece and I will see our guests meet her since you are involved with your duties here." Down the line a young fellow received a reprimand for wearing boots and was escorted from the hall. The duchess ignored the commotion and scanned the ballroom growing more crowded by the minute.

"There she is, Clarissa Downey, the lovely white dove speaking with Lord Blandon and his brother, Chester Buckley."

"The girl with the ghastly pallor, meager bosom, and thin hair? Has the poor child been ill?" the duchess asked with great concern.

"Of course not! Alabaster skin runs in our family." The patroness patted her coiffure as if to make certain her own thin brown locks had not come down from beneath her hairpiece.

"Yes, I had forgotten. Come along, we have many introductions to make." The duchess turned on her small heels and headed into the fray, a general about to do battle with her troops following her lead.

"Now you see what this place is like," James told the Hardacres.

"Never fear, my wife will guide you. She excels in matchmaking, wit, and bantering, seldom losing in a conversation. Still, I wish I weren't always blamed for my daughters' coloring. They are lovely just as they are." The duke pushed past several gentlemen trying to make their acquaintance, mowing them aside like tall grass before a scythe.

They arrived before the unfortunately pallid and somewhat scrawny tall girl standing beside and towering over Lord Blandon. There, the duchess kept her promise of introductions to her twins, her son and her houseguests. Lord Blandon's pale blue eyes lit upon meeting her daughters. He drew his brother forth immediately. "My brother, Chester Buckley."

They were definitely not identical twins. Chester possessed large, sad brown eyes like a hound often kicked aside but still hopeful of gaining a pat on the head. That head was covered with thick, curly brown hair that continued down the sides of his round, somewhat florid face, in thick and vigorous side whiskers. Barrel-chested Chet tended toward fat and Lord Blandon toward lean like Jack Sprat and his wife of the nursery rhyme, though both were turned out as well as a fine tailor could enhance them with a little padding here in the shoulders and a trifle more cloth there over the belly. Indeed, beside Chester, Lord Blandon seemed rather shrunken and slight. His pale hair already retreated from his temples though he was not over thirty, and his cheeks sunk in where his brother's puffed out.

The Earl of Blandon raised his thin lips in a smile of greeting. "An honor to meet such vibrant young ladies. Ah, Chet, to judge by the sparkle in their lovely brown eyes, we might have a pair of minxes on our hands tonight."

The duke bristled like the bears he was often compared to. "My daughters are not to be compared to minks, those vicious, sneaking weasels!"

Lord Blandon stepped back and Chester actually cowered. The duchess intervened quickly. "Not minks, my darling. He meant they might be pert or saucy, minx with an X on the ending."

"They are somewhat spirited," he conceded as he pulled his gloves back into place before actually committing a challenge to a duel.

"Then allow us to lead them in the first dance! Chet has never married, you know, and though I have known wedded bliss, I had not considered entering that state again after my poor, sickly bride went to her rest. These two might change my mind."

Again, the duchess intervened. "Their first two dances are promised to our guests, but certainly later. I am sure Clarissa would adore your leading her out, Blandon, and having Chester for her second partner.

"Oh, yes, delighted," the pale Clarissa said, peering over a few heads. She'd faded to the rear of the group that crowded around the triple sets of twins drawing the attention of the ton.

"Good, that is settled. I believe we can squeeze in one more introduction before the music begins." The petite, blonde general reconnoitered and set off in another direction.

"So good to see you again, dear Liza! Lady Mallet, allow me to introduce my daughters, Clio and Calliope who are coming out this Season. I see Angelique is also done with her schooling." The duchess inclined her head toward a young miss with a bountiful and alluring figure and as light of eye and hair as her twins were dark. The girl executed a perfect curtsy that disturbed not a lock of her fair and smoothly coiffed head.

"We are familiar with Clio and Calliope. They briefly attended Mrs. Pyncheon's Female Institute with Angelique," Lady Mallet said with a faint hint of disapproval in her voice and something judgmental in same blue eyes her daughter had inherited. She shook her head slightly without dislodging a curl of what the duchess always called Liza's unfortunate ginger hair, that color being quite unstylish at the moment. Luckily, her daughter tended toward the blond locks of the father, though Lord Mallet had lost most of his as he aged.

"Tell us, has Mrs. Pyncheon's hair grown back, Angelique? Really, it looked better shorn. She nearly resembled the Empress Josephine— without the great beauty, naturally," Clio inquired, showing some of that pertness.

"Yes, it has somewhat. She's always said she could have been murdered in her sleep instead of merely being scalped." Angelique's blue-eyed gaze strayed from the twins to the trio of handsome, eligible men standing with the duke as if she wanted to pluck a bonbon from a box of sweets and could not decide on which one.

Callie shrugged her shoulders and earned a disapproving glance from her mother. "As Papa would say, Mrs. Pyncheon wasn't scalped, she merely lost her braid. Nothing was ever proved against any of the girls. It might have been a burglar procuring hair for a wigmaker."

"Yes, one would think her female students would bring nothing sharper with them than sewing scissors, nor would they be so stealthy-footed," Lady Mallet said, never taking her eyes from Clio and Callie as if she expected to the extract the confession that poor Mrs. Pyncheon could not.

"Oh, I have neglected to introduce our guests, Gareth Hardacre, Viscount Marston, and his brother, Tristan Hardacre," the duchess exclaimed, deftly turning the conversation. "They are striking up the music. Dearest, let us make up a set, you and I, the girls with our guests and Angelique with James. Hurry now!"

The designated couples joined Callie promenade around the ballroom floor. As the first dance turned out to be one of the most familiar reels, sets were not needed and the Hardacres kept up without embarrassment or treading on feet. If they lacked grace, they made up for it in enthusiasm. With the dancers loosened up, the more complicated cotillion was called and the Longleigh family formed their set with the twins exchanging partners, James escorting his mother, and the duke the light-footed Angelique, who made a great show of being honored but kept her eyes on his son occupying the opposite of the square. When the ladies took a turn wheeling in the center, she stepped out too soon and reclaimed her place next to James.

"Oh my, what a silly error on my part," she claimed as the others were forced into a new arrangement, the duke with one of his daughters and the duchess with a Hardacre boy. One of the female twins, Clio judging by the wink of rubies in her hair, had kept her male counterpart, but neither of the sisters looked pleased.

As the music ended, the duchess began repositioning her cohorts. "James, quickly to Clarissa. Blandon and his brother are coming our way. Girls, you will dance with them no matter what your opinion. One of you…" she gestured toward the Hardacres. "Ask Angelique for a turn." That left her with her husband and a spare Hardacre. "No matter, whichever one you are, come with me, and we shall find you a new partner. Remember, no more than two dances with any young lady or people will talk, and it is far too early in the Season for that!"

"But Viscount Laughlin and I had only a dance and a half," Angelique protested.

"That is one half more than you shall get for the rest of the evening, my child. One of these lads is also a viscount. Good luck with finding out which. Dearest, I believe I require some liquid refreshment and will sit out the next dance."

All settled to her satisfaction, the duchess found an unoccupied chair and fanned herself as her husband fetched two cups of bland beverages and returned to sit beside her. "The ratafia or the orgeat?" he asked. "Both are equally poor."

"The orgeat, I suppose. That was close. Angelique nearly had her claws sunk into James before I wrestled him away." The duchess sipped her orange-flavored liquid.

"James is too crafty to be trapped into three dances, my love, but would Angelique be such a bad choice? She is certainly pretty enough and comes of a good family. I could inquire about her dowry. Bah, not enough spirits in this ratafia to even taste it!" The duke set his glass aside.

"No need to bother. She has eight-thousand pounds, perfectly adequate, and James doesn't need the money. I suspect he has more wild oats to sow before he settles down, and it is best to get that out of the way. I only wish he would stay in England to do that."

"Would you care for any of the miserable bread and butter or a slice of the pound cake, equally miserable?"

"Don't exert yourself to get it, Pearce. Why they feel they must serve such niggardly refreshments to prove how exclusive this club is and people will flock to it regardless, I do not know."

Two dances passed. "Time to be on our feet again and rescue the girls from Blandon and Chet, though I've never seen the latter more bright-eyed and jolly. Collect the Hardacres and we shall make more introductions. Where is James?"

The duke smiled knowingly. "He vanished sometime after a single dance with Clarissa. I told you the boy is wily. You did not see him go."

"But you did and failed to stop him?"

"He's a grown man. If he can find his way through the forest at Bellevue Hall after his Shawnee initiation rite, then he can manage to get back to the townhouse on his own. Another dance, my dearest?"

Seven

In the small hours of the morning, the ducal coach carried them all home again, minus the errant James. Clio and Callie nodded against their father's broad chest as he sheltered them with his brawny arms as an eagle does its hatchlings. The Hardacres flanked Lady Flora like duplicate Greek statues portraying youthful manliness cast from an identical mold. Both showed the stamina of young men out on the town for an evening. Upon arrival at Bellevue House, the duke gently patted his girls awake. They went off to their bed immediately without protest.

The duchess enquired of her butler about Lord James. "Home for some hours, Your Grace."

"Inebriated?"

"Not a bit, but smelling somewhat of strong perfume."

"I wish you had never introduced him to Chanel's place of business," she said to her husband as they ascended the staircase.

"The whores are clean, healthy, and inventive there. Would you rather he took his urges to a woman on the street and caught a disease?"

"Of course not. I'd rather he marry!" The duchess followed her husband to his chamber, making no pretense of sleeping apart as was the style.

~ * ~

The couple seemed to have forgotten their guests trailing behind them with their man, Oskar, ready to do whatever they required of him, though still unsure what those duties might be. Their manservant took a guess, stirred the fire, and lit the oil lamps placed around the bedchambers. In the greater illumination, the twins immediately noticed several tears in the new livery and a piece of ruching dangling from his breeches. Oskar's wig, somewhat muddied, would also require attention.

"Did you fall off the coach, Oskar?"

"No, milord. A few of those pretty jackanapes attending other carriages saw fit to jibe at me. They ain't so beautiful anymore." Oskar adjusted his eye patch worn a little askew. "Anything your lordships want before I get me rest?"

"Help us from these restrictive jackets. Otherwise, we will burst the seams trying to get out of them. After that, I think we can manage on our own."

Oskar carried out this small duty and left them alone. Gareth said to his brother as they unknotted each other's cravats, "I understand why James slipped away. I felt hunted the entire evening."

"By beautiful and wealthy maenads. I have no problem with that. Once they discover you are the heir, they will cease pursuing me. For the time being, I plan to enjoy the attention." Tristan sat on a stool with a needlepoint cover possibly rendered by the Lady Flora's own hand and removed his shoes and dark stockings.

"Would you like to have all the attention? I met none I fancy more than Lady Calliope. She is milder than her sister but still spirited, and if her mother bore ten living children, she is sturdy enough to meet even our father's standards. I would like to court her quietly as the second son and see if she responds." Gareth removed his waistcoat and shirt, exposing the smooth tanned skin he'd acquired sea bathing in the cove. He draped his clothes carelessly over a chair.

"What, not interested in the whey-faced Honorable Clarissa Downey or the bountiful Lady Angelique? I am tempted by the latter, though I certainly wouldn't cast aside Clio Longleigh and her twenty-thousand at this point. Not that any of them would have a second son." With his back to the fire, Tristan also removed his shirt and tossed it aside. After all that vigorous dancing it wouldn't do for another day.

"Then play the heir for a while. You've always been the more aggressive, and they will think that a sign of being the first born."

"Because I had to be to survive! Our father would have preferred me dead rather than deal with not knowing which of us was which. You can be as gentle as you like and your every word is still law at Castle Blackwater." Tristan turned and revealed a scar on his shoulder. It formed the number II and glowed red in the firelight. Gareth touched this old wound, and his brother flinched as if it were still raw and not healed for many years.

"I wish the old scoundrel had done the same to me."

"Well, he didn't."

"Take my place for our stay in London. We will announce that you are Viscount Marston tomorrow and wear some sort of symbol like the Longleigh twins. But, in the meantime, we should sleep in our shirts lest anyone in the household see the mark."

"Agreed, then."

The brothers removed the rest of their clothes and resumed the shirts. After all their exertions on the dance floor, they slept well and far into the morning.

Eight

At a very late breakfast, the Hardacre twins appeared refreshed but were the last to arrive at the table where Clio and Callie tarried, waiting upon their arrival. They'd taken some time to consider devices telling them apart and finally settled on ribbons exactly like the ones worn by the girls, only not in their hair of course.

"We believe we wore out our jest last evening and now plan to assume colors like the young ladies. I, Viscount Marston, will have something red about my person, and my brother will have blue," Tristan told the assembled Longleigh family. However, they were dressed identically as they spread butter on toast and slathered the bread with marmalade.

"We shall have to make some more purchases to keep the theme," Gareth replied mildly.

Clio, who wore a muslin morning gown patterned in cherries, sprang up without excusing herself from the table. "We will get you some of our ribbons, just a snippet, to pin on your lapels, won't we, Callie?"

"Certainly!'

They were gone before their mother could issue a reprimand on poor manners and returned nearly as quickly. Callie, clad in blue and white checked gingham, shyly approached the twin who had taken a place beside her at breakfast and claimed to be the second son.

"I could affix this to your lapel now if you wish, since blue is also my color and I am another second-born."

Gareth leaned toward her to make the mission easier and rewarded her with a smile. "Now, I can go forth into the world as Tristan Hardacre. Thank you, Lady Calliope. Your name is poetry to my ears."

James choked on the coffee he preferred to tea in the morning, but his mother merely patted his back and said, "A lovely and delicate compliment, surely the first of many my daughters will garner this Season."

Clio rushed to pin a red loop of ribbon to the supposed Viscount Marston and pricked herself. A small dot of blood marred his buff lapel. "Oh, I am so sorry!"

"No matter at all. I admire a woman who would shed her blood for me." The true Tristan grinned.

"I do believe I have lost my appetite," James declared. "Papa and I are off to Hyde Park for a ride. Will you accompany us, gentlemen?"

"That would be very agreeable," Tristan said, assuming the lead as an heir should.

Taking the finger she had injured from between her red lips where she sucked the blood away while Tristan watched avidly, Clio asked immediately, "Might we go riding with them, Mama?"

"We haven't enough mounts as only James and your father brought theirs. Besides, I plan to be at home today and expect both of you to sit beside me on the settee and receive our guests." The duchess bit into her crisp toast decisively.

"Couldn't we just go to the park for a stroll and watch them ride or take the carriage?" Callie pleaded.

"Tomorrow, perhaps. Not today."

"You do enjoy riding, then?" the man pinned as Viscount Marston said.

"Oh, so very much!"

"They enjoy careening about the countryside scattering sheep and unnerving coachmen," James replied for his sisters. "I believe they failed to learn to walk a horse, simply went right to trot and canter."

"That's my girls for you. Do you know, they never crawled as infants but got right up on their tiny feet and began to toddle?" the duke said with pride.

Clio put on her most amiable expression. "Tomorrow, we could borrow James' thoroughbred and your old Bosworth and go with the Hardacres, couldn't we, Papa?"

"Certainly not without a chaperone," their mother interjected. "Do not give them permission, Pearce."

"I've heard all that people do in the park is ride up and down on Rotten Row to show themselves off. You could sit on a bench and watch over us with Mama. I promise we wouldn't stray from the path." Callie made her brown eyes wide and soulful.

James snorted. "My thoroughbred would toss you off in a second, and old Boz could ignore such a slight creature on his back and go to cropping grass."

"Would not!" both twins exclaimed.

"Are we back in the nursery then, children? The answer is no for today. If you must ride while in London, your father can see about renting some appropriate mounts. I won't have you bobbing about on Bosworth or breaking your necks being thrown by Black Magic. He is far too young a stallion for you to control. Those are my last words on the subject. Now finish your breakfast and prepare to greet our visitors." The duchess, as usual, did have the last word.

The Hardacres observed the family spat with slightly amused expressions while they shoveled eggs, kippers, and deviled kidneys into their mouths and remembered to use their napkins at appropriate times. The girls picked at their meals until the young men had enough and went upstairs to put on riding attire. They followed close behind and immediately ran into an argument of another sort.

Finch barred Oskar from using the staircase. "You can't go down there. Use the servants' stairs! And just look at the condition of your livery, all tattered and torn. No decent footman would dare be seen in such condition." The maid accosted him like a tiny bird warning a crow away from her nest.

"Never said I was a decent footman, and never wanted to be one. I had to defend myself from those who thought they were better than me last night. I might add, I showed them who really *was* the better man." Oskar puffed out his chest and a button hanging on by a thread dropped to the floor.

Finch scooped it up in one graceful swoop. "Take your livery off then. Someone must mend your costume before you go out again, and I am handy with my needle."

"Right here?" Oskar, the large and terrible, blushed. He looked down upon the precise part in the center of her neatly coiled brown hair beneath its small lace cap. She took a step back to confront him with amused hazel eyes, large and not dark or bird-like at all.

"No, you great lummox. Go into the dressing room and put on the clothes you wore when you arrived as they have been laundered. Bring the livery to me, and the wig. I will see what I can do to prevent your masters from being embarrassed by your appearance." Finch made a shooing gesture with her small but capable hands. Oskar fairly fled in the direction of the Hardacres' rooms.

"And you, young ladies, to your chamber to make yourselves presentable for your mother's at home."

"We are presentable!" Clio protested.

"Acquaintances of the duchess will be bringing their daughters. I want you to outshine them all. Now off with you." Finch swept the girls before her in the opposite direction from the Hardacres and firmly shut a door behind them.

Guffawing, Gareth and Tristan followed in Oskar's path. "I believe Oskar has met his match, Gary."

"And I believe we have met ours." The false second son cast a longing look at the tightly closed door where the twin daughters had disappeared.

~*~

Lady Flora's drawing room overflowed with substantial older ladies towing marriageable daughters along like barges on the Thames.

A fairly large group of the merely curious had come calling as well. When the Hardacre twins did not make an appearance, the latter left in a timely manner. The others overstayed their welcome. Servants hurried to replace plates of dainty refreshments as one delicacy after another disappeared down well-bred maws like bread thrown into the midst of a flock of quacking ducks.

"Yes, yes. Gareth and Tristan Hardacre did reveal themselves to us at last. They agreed to wear colors as my girls do, red for the heir and blue for the second son, to avoid confusion," the duchess assured her audience. "Unfortunately, they have gone riding with my son and the duke in Hyde Park and most likely will not return until supper."

As intended, the information caused several pairings to rise, say farewell, and rush to their carriages in hopes of catching up with the new men in town on Rotten Row and peer at their ribbons. Lady Mallet and her Angelique remained behind, and after the room cleared, so did Clarissa and her mother, who was less well-placed in society than her sister, the grand patroness at Almack's. Clarissa tended to fade into the background and hadn't spoken a word other than a greeting since her arrival. Pushed to the rear by the great number of visitors, they now stepped forward to bask in the presence of the small but mighty Duchess of Bellevue.

Lady Mallet plucked another flakey-crusted tartlet from a tray and settled in to stay a while longer. Once she swallowed without dropping a crumb, she said, "Are you sure these Hardacre lads aren't deceiving you, dear Flora? I have heard twins are prone to such mischief." She set her stern gaze on the duchess's daughters who sat on either side of their mother with hands folded in their laps, their posture perfect, and the strain of staying still and minding their manners showing in their eyes. They hadn't dared to eat or drink anything.

"Possible, but why would anyone masquerade as a second son? The debutantes will simply avoid him." Lady Flora, dry from talking to so many, sipped her tea.

Clarissa surprised them all by saying, "At least we will not have that trouble with Lord Blandon and his brother Chester. They are so unalike. I wonder how that can be."

"In the same way that a female cat might mate with many and have black, white, and orange kits in the same litter. It is said that the late Lady Blandon was given to spreading her favors around and that Chester came into the world greatly resembling her coachman while the first born fortunately is the epitome of now deceased earl," Lady Mallet informed her.

That comment brought pale pink roses to Clarissa's otherwise pallid cheeks, but she listened avidly to this new information. Her mother, Baroness Downey, appeared as if she wanted to clap her hands over her daughter's somewhat large ears ruthlessly exposed by the tightness of her coiffeur drawn up as a bun atop the girl's head and unhidden by skimpy curls. "Should we really be making such remarks before innocent girls?"

The duchess weighed in on the subject. "Certainly even innocent girls know how kittens are conceived. My daughter, Viscountess Valls, has a house overrun with cats and when the females are about to make another batch they wail like babies to attract every tom in the city. I believe it is better to have some knowledge of such things before bringing a young lady up to London where wickedness abounds."

"Surely you are right, duchess," the baroness deferred, bowing a countenance unfortunately very like her daughter's plain features.

"Well, enough about the habits of felines. We must be going soon. However, I do want to personally present an invitation to you and your daughters, your son and his guests, as well as the duke if he would honor us with his attendance, to a very special frolic Angelique and I have devised." Lady Mallet removed a card from her reticule and handed it directly to the duchess. "I did notice the abundance of invitations overflowing on your hall table and did not want ours to be lost in the clutter."

The duchess accepted the card, "Ah, our presence is requested for an afternoon of refreshing activities to include playing with hoops, the Game of Graces, nine pins, and shuttlecocks to be followed by an informal supper."

"You see, I thought our daughters could show off their elegant forms in such activities. Perhaps we might have hobbyhorse races for the young men, and of course, they will join the young ladies in nine pins and shuttlecocks. Angelique is quite adept at all of these skills as I am sure Clio and Calliope are." Lady Mallet had issued another challenge.

The duchess picked up the gauntlet. "They do. We accept your kind invitation."

"I do not excel at these exercises, but it does sound like great fun," the Honorable Clarissa said with a voice painfully full of hope. She glanced toward the reticule as if it might produce another treasure like a genie's lamp.

"I am certain we shall see you there, will we not, Liza?" The duchess directed her gray stare at Lady Mallet.

"Your invitation must be on its way as we speak, Clarissa. I have a key to the square in front of our townhouse, and we shall have our frolic there weather permitting. If it is inclement, then we will go inside and enjoy an afternoon of music provided by the young ladies. Angelique has prepared several pieces, both vocal and on the pianoforte, if the occasion demands it. I know we can count on your daughters as well—a duet perhaps?" Lady Mallet said, as if vastly amused by the idea.

"They will be ready!" The duchess rose, taking all the others with her and moving them toward the door where the usual good-byes were exchanged.

Turning to her daughters, she said, "I will expect your best performances."

Freed at last from the constraints of the afternoon, the twins exhaled, but their dark brown eyes were alight with excitement. "A Longleigh never backs down from a challenge!" Clio declared.

"She stole my very words," Callie said.

Nine

As it turned out, no one but the men went for rides in the park. The duchess had a scant week to prepare her small soldiers for combat in tossing and chasing hoops and mastering the shuttlecock. To her great chagrin, she had never seen fit to put a bowling green in her small London garden, though Bellevue Hall possessed a very fine one used by guests during the grouse hunting season. She might have to settle for three out of four victories.

In the chilly March air, the twins warmed up quickly using their set of wooden dowels to send a small beribboned hoop flying back and forth between them until their arms tired. They chased hoops up and down the narrow walkways of the townhouse garden until their calves burned, their mama constantly cautioning them to avoid treading on the burgeoning tips of her tulips and daffodils.

Deep into bouncing shuttlecocks on their rackets both singly and to each other, their small faces began to show the first signs of mutiny. Callie nodded and flipped the feathered birdie to Clio who whacked it to the far end of the garden—where it bounced off the broad chest of the presumed Viscount Marston as he opened the gate from the mews. The men had returned from their ride and an afternoon of exercise at Gentleman Jackson's Saloon. They exuded a manly scent of leather and horses and honest sweat not at all unpleasant. Three pair of delicate female nostrils breathed it in with pleasure.

Grinning wickedly, Tristan caught the birdie in his hand and returned it to Clio with a bow. "I believe you have lost the game with such a wild hit."

"Oh, we've hardly begun to play yet. Would you like to join us if your exertions haven't tired you too much?"

"What do you say, Ga—Tristan?"

"If we were fatigued, the sight of your beauteous faces has restored us. James, are you feeling up to shuttlecocks?" Gareth asked with sympathetic concern.

Their brother, hat canted low, pushed by the group clogging the walkway. "I think not. See you at supper."

The duke joined his wife on a bench to watch the play—Clio to Tristan to Callie to Gareth and around and around again. Callie absently rubbed an aching elbow after tossing the shuttlecock to Gareth. He immediately dropped the birdie. "So sorry, I've broken the ring. Perhaps I am tiring. Shall we sit?"

"I would like that very much." Callie immediately spread her skirts on an empty seat and Gareth joined her, moving over slightly when the duke seemed to gauge the distance between them as too close with his glare.

"Marston, I am not at all tired. Let us continue." Clio passed him the birdie. They continued on for some time until he, too, missed his turn. Clio raised her arms in the air and, whirling, declared, "I am victorious!" She threw herself beside her sister and beckoned to Tristan to join them. Four on the bench made for elbow-rubbing and thigh-touching. The duke stood immediately and suggested they all go inside to rest and prepare for the evening meal. Voiced in a deep growl, the suggestion readily became an order. He drew the young men away from his daughters while his wife lingered behind.

"Clio, the point of the games is to show off your gracefulness, not to win. Men do not care for women who best them. Keep that in mind," the duchess chided her girls.

"Papa doesn't care. He encourages us to win," Callie pointed out.

"Your Papa is unlike other men in so many ways. Really, I don't know where the two of you get your competitive streak." She set off after the men.

"Yes," said Clio as she watched her mother march away. "I can't imagine where."

~ * ~

At the supper table, James did not take his accustomed place but sat in a shadowy area ill lit by the candelabrum illuminating the table. As the duke liked to point out, no use in igniting every candle in the chandelier when only the family dined. Finding the more intimate lighting flattering, the duchess did not disagree with him on this, but it did not prevent her sharp gray eyes from noticing everything that went on around her.

"James, will you be joining us at Lady Tiffin's fete this evening?"

"I think not, Mama." Her son answered without bothering to turn in her direction.

"Whatever are you doing way down there?"

"Eating my soup, Mama." James slurped loud enough to be heard the length of the table.

The Hardacre twins exchanged knowing smirks that roused the curiosity of both the duchess and her daughters. The duke merely continued to eat, sopping up the broth with a bit of bread.

"Come join the rest of the family and our guests immediately. Bring your soup with you."

When James failed to move, the duke chimed in, "You heard your mother."

Reluctantly, their son closed the gap between himself and the others. The better light exposed an empurpled, swollen eye on his handsome visage. Without comment, he resumed eating his soup.

"Which one of you did that to our brother?" Clio exclaimed with more glee than grief.

"I am afraid I am the guilty party," the false Viscount Marston revealed. "You see, when we engage in fisticuffs at Castle Blackwater, we fight in earnest in order to win or to survive. We don't play at it merely sparring for sport. I failed to pull my punch in time at Gentleman Jackson's this afternoon."

"I would have returned the favor if Papa hadn't stopped me," James replied, stiff and surly.

"A man should accept his blows without malice, my boy, at least in the saloon. Out in the streets or in self-defense, it would be a different matter. I take it Lady Tiffin skimps on the refreshments, my dear, as we are dining early." The duke motioned for a haunch of lamb to be set before him and carved it with finesse.

"There will be enough champagne to make young girls tiddly if they partake too much and lead to ugly issues if we stay overly long. Lord Tiffin never skimps on the wine as it is his chief delight in life, but one should not attend their affairs without dining first as a preventative to drunkenness." The duchess accepted a tender slice from the tip of his knife and doused it with mint sauce.

Not to be thrown off the trail, Callie, dark eyes gleaming at the Hardacres across the table, asked, "Which one of you bested James at chess when he stayed at Castle Blackwater?"

"That would be me," Gareth confessed. "But your brother is a wily opponent who defeated both my father and brother and very nearly had me also," he ended graciously.

James did not comment, but Callie continued, "And which of you loves dogs?"

"Both of us," they answered simultaneously.

Folding her hands beneath her chin, she beamed at them. "How perfect."

"Elbows off the table, Calliope. James, a bit of rice powder and some of my ointments would make you presentable. Won't you come with us?" the duchess pursued.

"No, thank you. I plan to spend the evening with a piece of beefsteak on my eye, not in stage make-up like our grandpapa."

"Have it your own way, then."

"I am sure we will have a glorious time without you," Clio could not forbear from saying.

~ * ~

The clock struck two but few heard its chimes at Lady Tiffin's crush. As the wine flowed, the voices grew louder and so did the music as the players strove to overcome the din. The duchess tugged on her husband's lace cuff to get his complete attention and lowered his ear closer to her mouth. "Time we left. The girls are giggling far too much and have been at the champagne, I can tell. Weren't you watching them?"

Mellowed by his own intake of wine, the duke shook his head. "Impossible. They whir about like identical hummingbirds. No way to keep an eye on them."

"There, they have latched onto the Hardacre boys again. I hope this is only the second dance with either."

"Who could tell?" Because of his great size, the duke held his liquor well, but there would come a point when the more savage side of his nature might make an ugly appearance. The duchess gauged that time to be about an hour away. Best to be going now.

She bustled over to the group of young people. "Get your wraps. Time to leave."

"Oh, but we are forming a square for the next cotillion with Angelique, Lord Blandon, Clarissa and Lord Chester. Can we not dance one more set?" Clio begged.

She wore a white gown fetchingly threaded through with red ribbons and more adorned her black curls. Callie was gowned in the same pattern of dress but with the blue ribbons accenting hers. She stood beside Gareth with the bit of blue ribbon she had provided ornamenting his lapel. Lord Blandon, escorting Angelique, headed their way with Chester and Clarissa trailing them as usual. The music began, and Clio seized Tristan's hand and dashed out onto the floor. The others raced to join them.

"Did you see how our daughter defied me, Pearce?" the duchess demanded of her spouse. "Stop them at once!"

The duke accepted another glass of champagne from a passing servant. "Surely one more dance cannot hurt." But it did. The duchess was nearly always right.

In the confusion Clio created, their square formed up with Chester beside Angelique and a flustered Clarissa beside Lord Blandon. From the flush on her cheeks and a thinning of her full lips, Angelique was none too happy with this outcome, but she carried on through the intricate steps, plastering a pleasant smile upon her face her until the women moved to wheel in the center.

As she had once before, she fell out of the circle one man too soon and claimed Tristan Hardacre as her new partner. Clarissa failed to respond soon enough and stumbled, only to be rescued and placed in the formation again by Chester who placed her next to the other Hardacre. "Oh la, I've misstepped again. Pardon me, Clarissa. Too much champagne, I fear." Angelique fanned her rosy cheeks with a gloved hand but made no move to return to Chet.

"You seem completely sober to me," Callie said from her place, now beside Lord Blandon.

"Yes, I want my partner back," Clio demanded.

"Too late, we shall be all in a tangle if I do that now, wouldn't you say, Lord Marston?" Angelique fluttered her lashes at Tristan who gave her an encouraging smile but not a reply.

The ladies were to meet in the center of the square and retreat with a light-hearted curtsy before linking elbows with their partners and turning about. As Angelique backed to reclaim her place by the supposed Marston, a small slippered foot kicked out from beneath red-beribboned skirts and sent her sprawling. Tristan caught her in his arms before she crashed to the ground, which only angered Clio more.

"So sorry. Too much champagne," Clio claimed in a strident voice more like a combatant than a penitent. "Now, return to your true partner."

As other couples turned to stare, the band ramped up the music to a higher pitch, hoping to cover this diversion from the dance. It did no good.

"I believe I shall remain with Viscount Marston who saved me from injury." Angelique employed her eyelashes again.

"Move or I will cut off those sausage curls beside your face." Clio's hand moved down her skirt. "If they are real, that is."

"It is Clarissa who has the thin hair and must augment it with false locks, not I," Angelique said with malice.

Standing beside Gareth and looking very lost beside the strapping young man, the poor woman colored to the very roots of her real hair well tucked beneath supplemental braids. "Perhaps I should escort you back to your mother, Miss Downey," her momentary escort offered.

"I should be glad to accept that role," Chester offered, poking out a crooked elbow toward Clarissa who seized it like a barnacle attaching itself to a large ship's hull. Chester used his bulk to push a pathway through the gathering crowd. The music petered out, and mouths grew silent as ears strained to hear every word of the argument.

"I will scalp you as I did Miss Pyncheon!" Clio began to raise her skirts.

"No, Clio, no!" Callie called out.

Another voice entered the argument. "You confess at last! And so, the Longleigh twins reveal their savage blood." Lady Mallet stepped in front of her precious daughter, but she had no need to protect her.

The Duke of Bellevue appeared in time to gather his twins tight against his sides in a loving yet unbreakable grip. "Your mama says it is past time to go home. Make your apology and give your curtsy, my little birds." His daughters managed a bob and uttered a "Sorry" while still in his embrace. One glare from their father's dark and burning eyes and the onlookers parted to let them pass.

Tristan Hardacre leaned toward Lord Blandon. "I've seen women brawl in taverns, but never suspected the same went on in the ballrooms of the ton." By the glitter in his sea blue eyes, he was not displeased by the event.

"Very rare, extremely rare," Blandon informed them. He lowered his rather nasal voice to a level of confidentiality. "It's said those tiny Longleigh bees do carry a sting in a form of a dagger beneath their skirts. They have that strain of red Indian blood, and it showed itself tonight. I fail to see who would want to marry them no matter what their dowry and no matter how tempting their appearance."

Whether he truly meant to warn the Hardacres or plotted to keep a twin for himself was difficult for the young men to decipher in the strange world of the ton. The early part of his speech seemed more intrigued about the girls than worried. "Oh, I believe their background might add some excitement to the match," Tristan answered.

"I can agree with that entirely," Gareth concurred. "If we are riding with the duke, we had best hurry along." Entirely pleased with their latest discovery, they made their bow and left Lord Blandon with a look of astonishment on his pale face.

Ten

The twins did not go riding in the park the next day. Clio, holding her head in her hands at the breakfast table, declared she could not endure the jostling of a horse, which comforted her because the duchess had set a rigid schedule for the day. First, her miscreant daughters would write sincere and elaborate letters of apology to Lady Tiffin for causing a scene at her fete and very belatedly to Miss Pyncheon for the loss of her hair. They would include a banknote for a hairpiece. After that, they'd receive callers no matter how boring with their mother and be perfectly polite. Following the visitations, each girl was scheduled to practice their piano and singing, one playing to accompany the other, and then contrive some charming duets in case it rained the day of Lady Mallet's gathering.

"Do not expect me to hit any high notes," Clio grumbled as she partook of only tea and toast.

Callie, not nearly as hung over, added eggs to her plate. Both perked up considerably when the Hardacre boys entered the room and displayed a lusty appetite for the breakfast offerings. They even laughed a little as James arrived and helped himself to coffee from the silver urn. He wore a black leather eye patch over his bruised gray eye.

"Have you decided to go to sea as a pirate?" Callie enquired, barely containing her mirth.

"I merely prefer patch to paint." Refusing to bicker, he filled his plate and took a seat near the rest of the men as if seeking the safety of masculine numbers.

"Wherever did you get it?" his mother asked as she passed him the pot of strawberry jam that sat in front of his father.

Gareth answered for him. "Oskar offered its use to Lord Laughlin. The leather patch is his Sunday best."

His mother made an assessment. "You look rather dashing, James. Will you be at home to greet our callers today?

"Heaven forbid! No, I plan to spend the day at the British Museum viewing the Towneley collection of Greek and Roman sculpture. Our houseguests are welcome to accompany me if they have any interest."

"What, not another day at Gentleman Jackson's saloon?" Clio said, unable to resist pricking her brother again.

"There is a time for fisticuffs and a time for culture. I believe London is blessing us with a rare sunny morning." He rose from his repast and flung open a set of curtains opposite Clio.

"My eyes!" She covered them with her hands.

"Yes, there are all sorts of visual disorders, aren't there?" James took his seat again and appeared to enjoy his breakfast even more with the light streaming across his bacon.

"Now that was cruel. Clio has a headache," his mother chided.

"She overimbibed champagne. Yes, I heard all about that from Marston and his brother. The girls were fighting over them with Lady Mallet's daughter. Most unbecoming. You should curb them, but no, Papa encourages them to run wild, and you have regaled them with stories of your youthful misdeeds practically from birth."

The duke glowered at his heir. "I teach them to be self-sufficient like young Shawnee women. They could survive in the wilderness if need be."

"They will never need to do that! We live in the most civilized nation in the world."

The duke's fist hit the table. Cups of coffee and tea sloshed over and metal utensils chattered against china plates. "Even now your sister, Iris, treads the wilds of America with that artist husband of hers. Do not tell me my daughters have no use for my training." He spoke in a tone that said perhaps his heir had also been given too much freedom.

Gareth Hardacre attempted to soothe the roiling tempers. "Really, we were flattered by the attention of so many lovely ladies and thought nothing of it."

In the end, the duchess meted out a subtle punishment for her son's behavior. "If you had been in attendance last evening, you might have helped. No matter what you do today, you will be with us at Almack's next week and at Lady Mallet's frolic after that. Your presence is mandatory."

James groaned and attacked a kipper as if the smoked fish had personally offended him. The duke asked for the return of the jam pot and grinned with satisfaction like a bear that had discovered a cache of honey.

~ * ~

Despite their need to tread lightly around the powerful Duchess of Bellevue, the Lady Patronesses of Almack's grouped together for security and laid down their law. If the Longleigh girls could not show decorum within the sacrosanct walls of the club, they would be banned for the duration of the Season.

"I perfectly understand," said Lady Flora, fanning with such vigor she sent sharp whaps of air into their self-satisfied faces and stirred the feathers in their hair. "Lady Tiffin has accepted their apology and did say the small incident added zest to her fete. My children are welcome to attend any future gatherings at her home. Of course, if my girls are unwelcome here, my son will not be attending either."

James, standing at her side as she'd ordered before alighting from their carriage, did not mind being used as a threat. He admired his mother immensely when her tongue cut as sharp as a sword in defense of her family. If his sisters were banned, he would not mind that so much either. No more of these immensely boring affairs for him.

With that, the duchess led her dangerous daughters forth to fill their dance cards, which they did with alacrity. Men, it seemed, craved some spice added to the bland offerings of Almack's. The duchess required her son to dance in every set where his sisters participated. Heir to a duke and handsome enough to win a masculine beauty contest with the Greek statues he'd gone to see at the British Museum, he also had no problem finding partners. The eye patch peaked curiosity, but he merely replied, "A slight mishap soon mended." Whispers went round about the small scar high on his cheek, earned in a duel abroad the gossips said, a man even more hazardous than "those wild girls." Women young and old swooned for him if he so much as passed near them.

Unable to avoid it, he found himself partnered with the Lady Angelique, her having completed her dances with Lord Blandon who could make her a countess, and Marston whose wife would become a marchioness. She worked her way up the hierarchy. His status trumped them all, and he knew it. Angelique was unlikely to attempt the partner switch again and set off Clio who had pledged to two dances in a row with Blandon. Callie dutifully accepted a turn with Chester, and poor Miss Downey stood nervously next to the lesser Hardacre whose stature and vigor appeared to cow her. Marston, sitting this one out, entertained a coterie of young ladies with his dubious wit, most likely telling tales of sheep wrestling or some other rustic sport, James suspected.

Repressing his boredom and a sigh, James made his bow and entered the dance. At the end of the set, the orchestra called for an intermission in the music. Immediately, Lord Blandon offered Clio his arm and suggested they go for refreshments. That left him no choice but to make the same offer to Angelique. Chester and Callie followed with Hardacre gallantly escorting Clarissa, no matter what his feelings on the matter. As usual, the meager offerings were set out in a room too small to accommodate the crush. Chester, adept at making his way to tables of food, offered to obtain refreshments for everyone while James and Hardacre got in line for the weak beverages. As they inched forward toward the orgeat bowl, James scanned the overheated chamber for Clio and found her nowhere. He excused himself and let his houseguest take over the duty of watering all the stock.

Backtracking, he searched the ballroom. Purposely, there were few places for a couple to hide from the patronesses and sharp-eyed mothers. He took a hallway that branched off toward the card rooms where his father had escaped earlier. Nothing much to see there except a potted palm and some dusty draperies covering a window at the end of the corridor. He nearly left before noticing the trembling of the palm fronds and a puff of dust from the curtains. Much as he mocked his father's training in woodland survival, though he'd loved it as a boy, he knew the twitch of a leaf or a sudden movement of air could reveal a wild beast or an enemy. He strode the length of the hall and ripped back the curtain to find Lord Blandon with his hand on Clio's breast and her hand pressing a stiletto against his side deeply enough to pierce the superfine wool of his jacket.

James groaned inwardly. He forced himself to utter the words, "Unhand my sister, Blandon. Clio, turn your back and put your knife away." Surprisingly, his sister obeyed. After she righted her dress, Clio swiveled, displaying the eyes of a doe frightened by the pursuit of a hound.

"Do you wish to marry this man, little sister?"

"No!" The ruby drops in her ears swung wildly as she shook her head. Every curl on her head trembled in denial.

"She came with me willingly. I like a spirited woman, but not an untamed savage who would stab me in my sleep. I have no more interest in her," Blandon claimed. Slender and sinuous of form and no match in any way for a Longleigh, he slipped from between James and his sister and tried to move away.

James seized his arm in a grip that would have made his father proud. In fact, he felt the duke's potent brand of anger rising within him. Where had that come from? "Say no more about my sister!"

"He said he wanted to show me a new and amusing card game, then swore as he pawed me that my reputation would be ruined if I cried out. Believe me, if you had not come along, I would have driven the blade between his ribs."

"You know what this means, Blandon. Have the grace to stay in one place and not run off while I remove my gloves. I am highly adept with a variety of swords and pistols. Choose whichever you like, but my sister's honor will be vigorously defended. You have gotten your heir already, am I correct? Perhaps Chester will stand in your stead as a guardian to raise him."

There were two kinds of warfare he remembered his papa saying, sheer savagery in the attack, but before that war cries of such pitch and volume that the enemy's mind quailed and his arm wavered. While not issuing any terrifying shrieks, his chosen words had the same effect. Beneath his fingers, Lord Blandon shook and the crotch of his snug knee britches dampened.

Unfortunately, the quiet corridor suddenly filled with a party of four done with gaming for a while. One of them was Clarissa Downey's aunt, the dreaded Lady Patroness. "What goes on here?" she demanded. She made for the curtain where Clio still stood in its folds and revealed her to all. "You again! You are a disgrace to your sex, young lady."

Although Clio's stance remained defiant, James thought he saw tears gathering in her large brown eyes. He dropped his hand from the earl's sleeve. "There is nothing disgraceful to be seen here. Intent on entering the card room, we paused to peer out the window to see if it rained. Blandon snagged his jacket on the palm, and my sister tried to extricate him without damaging the garment. Women are so much better at these delicate matters."

The Lady Patroness eyed the stain on Lord Blandon's breeches, but quickly averted her gaze. The earl rushed to explain. "I spilled some ratafia on myself earlier and desired to sit down until it dried. Isn't that right, Laughlin?" His desperate light blue eyes offered a compromise. He would not mention Clio's indiscretion in exchange for his life.

The patroness sniffed the air and breathed in the scent of urine and acute tension. "It is not ratafia you reek of, Blandon, but I will take your word on it. Disperse at once."

Lord Blandon did not hesitate to scuttle immediately into the card room and take a vacant seat. James offered his arm to his sister, who blinked her eyes several times, threw back her small shoulders, and steadied herself with his help. "I find I am no longer in the mood for cards. Shall we join the others for refreshments?" he prompted.

Clio managed a quivering smile. "That would be delightful." They promenaded down the corridor and back to the ballroom where they found the others gathered around the duchess as she held court in one of the roped off areas. The musicians returned to their stand and announced their next selection. Chester led Clarissa away, and the gentlemen who had secured the next dances with the twins arrived to claim their partners. The Hardacres, having had their two dances, departed to find unattached maidens. James supposed he must escort the young lady his mother had committed him to, but first he whispered in Lady Flora's ear. She nodded calmly, not showing an iota of chagrin, and moved off to find her husband. In a respectable period of time, she would claim a headache and withdraw her family from the fray without it looking one bit like a hurried retreat.

Eleven

"I tell you, Gary, I am having the best time of my life. It's good to be the heir. Women fawn over me. The beautiful and passionate Lady Clio nearly came to blows with the equally lovely Angelique vying for my favors. Even the art is more interesting here than at the castle with all those tattered tapestries and dour statues of saints. Why, I've never seen so many unclothed voluptuous female forms at we did at the British museum, not even in a brothel, and a man can stare as long as he likes in the name of admiring the works of antiquity without paying excessively for the privilege. If I were truly you, I'd stay in London year-round and do nothing but spend the old man's money." Tristan Hardacre stood to allow Oskar to help him into his jacket.

"We have obligations to our tenants at home, the sheepherders, the fishermen. Castle Blackwater needs shoring up, and Papa doesn't lift a finger to improve it. Besides, the best people return to their estates in the late summer and stay there all winter hunting grouse and such." Oskar adjusted Gareth's neckcloth and completed an especially fine knot of his own devising.

"Do you have any idea why we left Almack's early last evening? I'd just made some new and charming acquaintances. Ah well, another tasty breakfast awaits us and not a bowl of porridge in sight on the sideboard." Tristan, thoroughly enjoying his role, led the way from the dressing room.

"Something unpleasant occurred during the break in the music. While all the Longleighs acted as if nothing untoward was going on, I've never seen Laughlin so grim. He could barely spare a smile or a civil answer to his partners afterward. I wouldn't twit the man anymore about the blows you've given him. He will be prepared now and beneath that gentlemanly exterior, I sense a dangerous man. Several of my partners said he dueled regularly when abroad and only received that one scratch on his cheek." Oskar stopped Gareth from leaving the bedchamber while he checked the jacket for lint.

"Exactly, he's been abroad. No one really knows what he did there. Women have overheated fancies about him," Tristan declared.

"Maybe it's the eye patch that attracts them. Always worked well for me with the ladies," Oskar said, finally stepping away and letting his charges leave for their meal.

The Hardacres entered a silent breakfast room. The entire family sat at the table not touching a morsel and allowing both tea and toast to go cold as they passed around a letter.

"The nerve of them! None signed their names, simply The Lady Patronesses of Almack's," the duchess fumed.

The spark back in her eyes, Clio said, "We know who put them up to it—Clarissa's aunt. She wants less competition for her niece. We should snub the girl!"

"That would be as unfair as what they are doing to you," Callie pointed out. "Poor Clarissa has enough problems with her long form, her skimpy curls and a dowry of only five-thousand. We should go out of our way to be kind to her and shame her aunt."

"Five-thousand seems sufficient to me," the false heir said. "Would it be intrusive to ask what that missive contains?"

"Clio has been banned from Almack's for conduct unbecoming a well-bred young lady," James informed them. "Although some of the patronesses witnessed her dramatics at Lady Tiffin's soiree, only Clarissa's aunt could possibly condemn her for being found hiding in a curtain with man who led her astray. She is, after all, an innocent. I offered to kill Blandon for my sister. Then the old witch intruded and drew her own conclusions though we quickly fabricated a tale about his coat being caught in a nearby palm. Ah well, let's look on the bright side. We do not have to set foot in Almack's again for the rest of the Season." Cheerfully, James knocked the end off a boiled egg and spooned out the yolk.

Clio crumpled a piece of cold, stiff toast into breadcrumbs. "Thank you, brother, but I'd rather have killed the man myself. I only regret destroying Callie's season as well."

"Not so! Only you are banned. Why, we could change the colors of our ribbons and take turns attending. No one would know the difference," Callie insisted.

"I would. Though you are very much alike, Lady Clio's attitude is much different, and she would give herself away," the false Marston said.

"You disguise it well, but you favor your left hand and have a tendency to twist your curls, Lady Calliope," Gareth added. "But perhaps, being twins we are more aware of subtle differences."

"If Clio is banned, none of us will attend." The duchess laid down her own law. "The girls are perhaps too immature to handle London society at the age of seventeen and should have been held back another year. Since we are here, we shall enjoy the opera and the art exhibits, the theater, musicales and soirees." At the head of the table, the duke attempted to hide a wince behind a cup of coffee.

"Lady Mallet's frolic is coming up, and she will not dare to retract her invitation. James, if you attend a ball, you will not dance with any young misses related to the Lady Patronesses," she continued.

"You have my word on that, Mama." He beheaded a second egg as carelessly as Henry the Eighth did a wife.

"Of course, our guests are not banned from Almack's and may attend if they wish," Lady Flora amended.

At his wife's words, the duke raised his great head and stared at the young men. Unmistakably, he sent a message as clear as the one on paper that neither would court his daughters if they chose not to stand with the family. They received his unspoken words and hastened to answer.

"I have no desire to go to Almack's if the charming Longleigh twins are not in attendance," Gareth insisted. Tristan hesitated a bit before agreeing, "Nor I."

"Then all is settled. We will enjoy the other pleasures London has to offer."

"Would that include a visit to Madame Tussaud's traveling exhibition of wax figures? A boy gave me a handbill as we left the British Museum the other day," Gareth said.

"Yes, I understand she displays the head of Marie Antoinette made from her death mask," the true Tristan said, displaying fresh enthusiasm for city life now that Almack's had been swept from the table.

"If that is what you wish to see, we should all go. Who knows, next year Madame Tussaud might show the heads of the Lady Patronesses." That said, the duchess gave her own boiled egg a decisive whack of her spoon and sent shards of shell scattering across the breakfast cloth.

Twelve

Being held on the cusp of April, Lady Mallet's frolic began at noon once the sun burned through the fog and dried the grass of the square, making it fit for the delicate slippers of the ladies. The hostess herself unlocked the gate to the private park near her townhouse and stationed her footmen to keep out the riffraff of London. Still, spectators stood a safe distance away to watch the ton at play.

While Lady Mallet flaunted her keys, the Duchess of Bellevue made sure none forgot her own status by regaling the company with a recounting of their visit to Madame Tussaud's Wax Museum where the proprietress herself greeted the ducal coach and showed them not only the tableau of the former French royal family and the Chamber of Horrors, but allowed them to view some new figures in the making, one a tribute to the late Lord Nelson. She highly recommended the display.

Lady Mallet returned the attention to herself by calling for the first of the games to begin. The young ladies lined up and chased their hoops across the lawn, guiding them deftly with beribboned wands. While neither the twins nor Angelique allowed their hoops to drop to the ground, the winner surprised them all. Clarissa Downey, longer in the leg than the twins and lighter in build than Angelique, won by several paces and received the first chaplet of posies from the hands of her hostess. Chester led a round of huzzahs while Lord Blandon clapped his hands politely.

Next up—hobbyhorse races for the young men. James Longleigh attempted to hide behind a stout tree, leaning casually against it as if simply enjoying its shade, but his mother drew him out and whispered one word in his ear. "Win!"

"It's a ridiculous game, Mama. Now if we raced real horses, I'd join in a minute."

"Get out there and show off. The more desirable you are, the sooner the ban will be lifted from Clio."

Grumbling, "What I do for the family," James took his seat on one of the wheeled wooden horses who had names painted in gilt on their necks. His creaking black mount bore the designation of Saturn, which fit his mood entirely. Blandon rode a red Cupid and Chester boarded gray Jupiter like a man about to overset a rowboat. Chet soon bogged down, the wheels sinking in the grass beneath his weight. James, made uncomfortable by his height greater than the other men, dug in his boot heels and did his best, his strong thighs pumping beneath their buckskin. The Hardacre twins, also handicapped by their stature, propelled Castor and Pollux as best they could. In the end, despite rallying cheers from the Longleighs, Lord Blandon by virtue of his short, lithe form won a mere nose ahead of James with Gareth and Tristan on their tails.

For some reason, obvious enough but unexplained, Lady Angelique crowned the triumphant Blandon with a laurel wreath as she said breathlessly, "How fast you are!"

"Indeed he is," James agreed, moving off to avoid shaking the hand of a man he despised. "Sorry, Mama. I shall redeem myself when they get to archery, a real skill, not a childish one.

Lady Mallet lined up the girls for the Game of Graces. Clio and Callie smiled with confidence. They were so attuned to each other no one could beat them at it—except Angelique's mother parted them and put them against her daughter and Clarissa. Clarissa soon dropped the small hoop tossed her way by Callie as if she hadn't seen it coming at her clearly. Angelique caught hers adeptly time after time. Clio, so intent on beating her, narrowed her eyes and gritted her teeth. Other pairs dropped out and turned to watch. She would have won, should have won, if Lord Blandon hadn't cried out, "Careful of that bee, Lady Clio." Her instincts told her to wave it away and in doing so, she failed to catch the hoop on her sticks and let it drop to the ground. Angelique accepted the floral chaplet from the hands of her mother with a proud smirk on her face.

"What's next? Our family is not faring well," the duchess asked.

"Men's archery, then the ladies," James answered her.

"Ah, archery. Perfect!" She knew who would decline to compete but would be the first to perform. The cry of "Bellevue, Bellevue, Bellevue!" rose in the spring air, the sound as sweet as bird song to her ears.

Her mighty husband held up his hands. "An exhibition only. My dear, if you would hold my jacket." He shrugged easily from his outmoded greatcoat and called for a quiver of arrows and a bow to suit his size.

"Isn't it thrilling seeing a man in his shirtsleeves?" Angelique whispered in the center of the knot of ladies.

"Considering they are still in their waistcoats and choking on their high cravats, all but the duke, I'd say they are hardly in a state of undress." Again, Clarissa surprised with this frank comment.

"Those who are more experienced can imagine the rest," the duchess said, never taking her eyes off her brawny husband.

Waving the target back a few more yards, Pearce Longleigh drew one arrow after another in rapid succession, all six of them crowding the bull's-eye in the end. Many in the ton had seen this performance before and when invited to hunt with the duke watched him bring down a deer with the same instrument, but the Hardacres clapped especially loud for the feat.

"You must school us in this sport," one of them insisted.

"A skill learned early among the Shawnee where you might not eat if you could not send an arrow into the heart of a stag," His Grace demurred.

Tristan and Gareth vied to go first, but having strength and no training, sent their arrows far and wild, some landing beyond the fence and scattering the gawkers. Lord Blandon and Chester both performed decently as did a few others, but James Longleigh, having observed and heard all the feminine chatter, intentionally went last. He notched his first arrow and turned it slowly toward the target with a definite hesitation in the direction of Lord Blandon who took immediate refuge behind the bulk of his twin. Laughing, James completed his circuit and duplicated his father's performance. The duke was the first to clap him upon the back. "My boy!" he said with pride.

Angelique glided up with the laurel wreath, fluttered those lavish lashes of hers and said, "My goodness, you are so tall I must stand on my tippytoes to crown you."

Before she could "accidently" rub her bosom against him, James bowed his head to her level. One of the many things he'd learned abroad was how to avoid the snares of husband-hunting women.

In women's archery, as James could have predicted, the twins triumphed with identical scores in the center of the target. The other young ladies might as well have sat this round out. Grudgingly, Lady Mallet raised the wreath. "Which one of you shall have it? I did not count on any ties."

"We will share as we do with everything. Callie first," Clio suggested. She applauded her sister's crowning. "What is our next event, Lady Mallet?"

"Nine-pins. I've had my men at work grooming a green for this occasion for weeks." The hostess looked up at the sun beginning to hide behind pale clouds like a modest maiden beneath a veil. "We must hurry and allow the young ladies to go first. There will be time enough for the men to play later if the weather permits."

As the duchess and her daughters told James they suspected, Lady Angelique had been practicing and held the advantage. Not only did her voluptuous form show off to complete advantage as she stooped low to roll the ball, but she perfectly placed each shot to take down only the most high scoring pins and left little for those following.

In frustration, Clio knocked down the redhead pin in the center and earned a penalty. She stomped off in pique muttering, "There was no bee, none at all," to any who would listen. Lady Mallet placed the second coronet on her daughter's blonde head and cast a triumphant smile in Lady Flora's direction.

"Enough, Clio. Show grace in defeat," her mother cautioned, returning the smile with confidence. "There is still shuttlecocks to come if the rain holds off." She cast her gaze toward the heavens where the clouds had thickened from a veil to a wooly gray blanket. The women around them began seeking the wraps they had shed earlier in the day.

Lady Mallet clapped her hands for attention. "Quickly, our last game. Take up your battledores, young ladies and gentlemen. The last to drop the shuttlecock is proclaimed the winner. Then we shall adjourn for our dinner." She shooed her youthful guests into a circle and gave Angelique the shuttlecock to start the game. The girl hit it at a slant to Clio, who managed to catch it nonetheless and pass it along to the next person.

Above the park, one particular cloud took on a bruised appearance as nasty as James' blackened eye. Droplets began to fall. The gentlemen missed on purpose to gallantly hurry the game along and perhaps to spare their fine hats by taking refuge under the trees. The less determined girls also dropped out quickly and took shelter as the rain began to spot their muslin gowns, but Clio, Callie, and Angelique played on with their strikes becoming stronger and far from friendly. The grass beneath their feet grew slick. Callie slipped and missed the birdie, its feathers becoming bedraggled in the beginning of a downpour. She went to stand beneath the duchess's umbrella brought from their carriage by a footman. The drops swelled in size and number. The maidenly white gowns of the combatants grew more and more transparent and still the two girls battled.

Most of the guests made for the townhouse or the shelter of their carriages, but the Hardacre boys, several very interested young men and all the Longleighs stayed to watch the ending. Water poured from all three vents of the duke's laced-edged tricorne. Thunder rumbled. Lightning stuck one of the larger trees in the square and filled the air with splinters and ozone. Ducking, Angelique missed Clio's return serve and conceded the victory as she fled toward the house.

Lady Mallet rushed forward and mashed the last of the floral wreaths on Clio's straggling black curls. "Take it before we all are killed! I never should have included archery where your savage blood could come to the fore. Oh dear, oh dear, Angelique shall die of a chill. I must see to her at once." She dashed for her own door with a footman keeping pace with an umbrella to shelter his mistress. She'd divested herself of the iron keys to the square at the first hint of lightning.

That left only the Longleighs and their houseguests in the park. Laughing at the storm, they made their way to the carriage. Ensconced inside and on their way to a warm hearth and their own hot dinner, Clio pouted, "Angelique won twice, but she had Lord Blandon's help."

"All of my children received a coronet, and if Lady Mallet had planned her frolic better, we would have brought home four. I am completely satisfied with all of you. Not even lightning stops the Longleighs!" the duchess declared.

All this foolishness to pass idle time and pursue a mate. James shook his head like a dog shedding rain drops. Still, he felt his mother's pride in the family's prowess. *Yes, good to be a Longleigh.*

Thirteen

The Hardacre twins slept well after the rigors of the frolic from archery to hobbyhorse riding and a hot supper which the duchess assured them was superior to anything Lady Mallet would have served. They slid beneath their covers and were out as the rained poured on the slate rooftop and the wind sent small puffs of smoke into their chamber from the briskly burning fire.

Oskar stayed up, drying out their fine new garments and brushing their stylish beaver hats back to their former luster. From time to time, he stepped out to confer with Finch on advice about preventing shrinkage of woolen jackets already tightly worn. By rights, he should have consulted the butler, but hated to let such a snob of a man know he had little knowledge about being a valet, let alone a footman. Finch never derided his efforts to improve himself, no matter what she thought of him.

"So, your young ladies are well, no sign of them taking a chill?" he asked her after practical matters were put out of the way.

"For all their small size, the twins are rarely ill. They take after the duchess in that way. I believe I heard the duke snuffling as he came up to bed. He doesn't accept sickness well and can be quite a bear about it." Finch paused before broaching a delicate subject. "Have your young men shown any preference for either Clio or Callie?"

"Oh, they are very taken with both—and the Lady Angelique."

"It will be hard to separate the pair if your charges decide on only one of them. I doubt they would accept an individual proposal at all."

"If only one were to go to Castle Blackwater, would you come along as her maid?" Oskar stared at the toes of the best pair of shoes he'd ever owned, shined so well he could see his eye patch and brutish face beneath the ridiculous wig.

"That would depend on many things: the pleasure of the duchess—and my own thoughts on the matter. I might someday work my way up to housekeeper with my own set of rooms if I remain here. Has Castle Blackwater a competent housekeeper?" If Oskar had raised his head, he would have noticed she tried to catch his eye, the remaining good one.

"The castle has none at all and is sorely in need of the service. You might get a chance to see for yourself. A message came from Lord Blackwater while all were out getting soaked, an invite I believe, but with the ruckus afterward I forgot to give it to me boys."

"You really should refer to them as Lord Marston and Lord Tristan."

At that, Oskar did raise his head and let out a laugh that might have wakened less sound sleepers. "I taught the lads their swordsmanship and how to wrestle. At times, they seem more like mine than Blackwater's sons."

"I do know that feeling. I rocked the girls in the nursery when they were only babes."

The conversation would have gone on longer if Oskar's bellowing laugh had not drawn the attention of Busby, shutting up the house for the night. "To your quarters, Finch. And this sorry excuse for a valet, also," he ordered. Though Oskar clenched the big fists that could strangle an ox and carry it home for dinner, they had no choice but to obey.

~ * ~

As the Hardacre twins dressed in the morning, their talk was all of the frolic.

"Did you see how transparent their gowns became when soaking wet like the whores in the village bawdyhouse who spray theirs to gain attention?" Tristan asked, still excited by the notion. "The Lady Angelique had more to show but Clio's raised nipples on those apple-sized breasts had their own appeal. How they wobbled bashing that shuttlecock back and forth. You'd never see that in Marston."

"I noticed but looked away," Gareth replied primly. "A lady should not be desired for her bosom alone. Her gentility and kindness must count for more."

"Ah, always Gareth the Good. Of course, once Clio discovers that I am not you, she will shift her affections. You should take her. She has the spirit to face down our father in domestic matters and could make our lives a great deal softer at the castle."

"Lady Calliope is not without spirit and would rule with a gentle hand."

"Ah, stuck on her, are you?"

Oskar cleared his throat, a rumble like last night's thunder. "I have it on good knowledge that the young ladies will not be separated. It will be both or none."

"I'd cleave to Clio, but know she has her heart set on the heir. Gareth is the only man I'd step aside for."

Gareth clapped his brother on the back. "Then it is good I prefer the milder one."

Oskar fumbled in his garish livery and drew out a letter. "Came yesterday from your father. Best have a look at it before you finish parceling out the sisters."

Gareth took it as was his right since it came addressed to him alone. He read his sire's scrawl with a face becoming more and more downcast. Then he turned it over to his brother.

"Might I ask your lordships what the old man says?" Oskar inquired, looming over their shoulders.

Though both raised their eyebrows at being called "lordships," Tristan began to read aloud the note as crude as his father's handwriting.

> *To Gareth, my son and heir,*
> *You and your brother both have had enough time to cull a bride from the herd. I can see no reason for you to linger in London spending my money on fine garments and fripperies any longer. If you have not made up your minds, bring the lot of them to Castle Blackwater and trot them by me. I will make the choice if you cannot. Consider this an invitation for the ladies to enjoy my hospitality. I expect the bunch of you within a week's time or come home by yourselves and seek elsewhere for a less particular wife.*
> *Phineas Hardacre, Lord Blackwater,*
> *yr. Father and Master*

"Such a gracious invitation, how could any lady refuse?" Tristan said wryly.

"We can only tender it to them in more gracious words. If they refuse, we shall still have to return home by his order. No place else on earth will I find another like Calliope." Gareth gave what could only be interpreted as a lovelorn sigh.

Oskar slammed him hard on the back. "None 'o that now. Your father was brave enough at sea and saved me life a time or two as I did his, but if ye show yourself weak for a woman, he'll be sure to choose another to teach you a lesson in manhood. I'd invite all ye can get to go along, and let the Longleigh ladies shine like juicy dark berries among brambles. Go on, see who ye can round up on your visits today."

Having little choice, the Hardacre twins went down to breakfast to tender the invitation to the Longleigh sisters. They found the family gathered as usual this time of day partaking of hot rolls, perfectly cooked eggs, slices of ham, and all the tea and coffee they could wish. If only Castle Blackwater could offer the same.

As the presumed heir, Tristan made the invitation, dressing it up as nicely as the platter of ham garnished with parsley and whole preserved apricots. For a moment, quiet enveloped the group. It was broken as the duke held in a massive sneeze long enough to get a handkerchief embroidered with his coat of arms to his nose. "Pardon," he said.

"I am afraid we cannot possibly accept this invitation at the moment," the duchess answered. "We have numerous invitations, and it is best our daughters attend these events. I also fear the duke is succumbing to an ague and cannot possibly travel, let alone through the marshes. Perhaps when the season ends, we might accept Lord Blackwater's kind invitation."

"You see, our father demands we return home within the week. We hoped to have your company to lighten our departure," Gareth explained.

"Oh," said Callie, sitting beside him. She raised a hand to her lips and very nearly put it down again atop of his. "Your visit has been much too short. Mama, are you certain we cannot accept their offer?"

Gareth spread his hand and his pinkie brushed hers ever so slightly. This did not go unnoticed by the duchess. "I am very certain we cannot go, but also very sorry."

The words had barely left her mouth when Busby entered to announce an extremely early caller. His distaste showed on his already dour face. "Lady Tartte wishes to see you immediately, Your Grace."

Lady Flora closed her eyes as if gathering the strength to endure torture. "That woman! She appears like a bird of ill omen bearing gossip in her beak as if it were a piece of carrion. She has certainly brought bad luck to two deceased elderly husbands. I wonder that Lord Tartte still lives."

"A blonde woman, well-formed and with unusual green eyes and a somewhat flirtatious manner—I believe we danced with her at Almack's," Tristan said.

"Make that a questionable blonde with tightly fitted garments who places herself among the maidens to attract partners while her decrepit husband plays at cards. My daughter, Iris, has a cat with eyes exactly that same unappealing shade of green. Regardless, I must see her. She always presages a piece of bad luck for the Longleighs." The duchess stood and the gentlemen rose with her, but she waved them back to their meal.

"Should we go along?" Callie asked.

"No, I will bare all after I have seen her."

"Do you want my company, Mama?" James volunteered. "Lady Tartte and I are acquainted from my time at Oxford when she was married to a patron of my college. Indeed, she patronized many of the young men."

"Then, no. I am sure she would like to offer you her—support once more. Let her find another." The duchess bustled from the room eager to get the interview over.

~ * ~

Lady Tartte sat by a small fire in the drawing room and had already been supplied with piping hot tea to ward off the brisk morning air that the storm dragged in its wake. Showing far too much bosom barely covered in pale green fabric like the shade of her eyes, she stood and made her curtsy to the duchess.

"Sit," Lady Flora said. "What brings you here before we have digested our breakfast properly?"

"My dear Lady Flora, I had to be the first to reach you. I attended Lady Mallet's frolic yesterday."

"I did not see you there."

"Alas, Lord Tartte felt the oncoming storm in his joints and required me to stay by his side indoors to help him hobble about. Not that I minded as I am well past the age for childish amusements."

"Yes, you are," the duchess agreed pleasantly and took a secret joy in seeing her guest's mouth tighten.

"Having no daughters to bring forward at the moment, I only watched a bit from an upper window. I remember your eldest son well from my days of living near Oxford with my second husband. What a manly display he, and of course your husband, put on with the bow and arrow. Such a comely young man, Lord Laughlin." Those cat-like pale green eyes turned dreamy.

"Did you come here to reminisce about James' university days, or have you something else to discuss?" the duchess reminded her sharply.

"Yes, I see I have gotten off the path. My, the state you were all in by the end of that affair! The girls racing for your carriage in their sodden gowns with the floral wreaths upon their curly heads like wild bacchantes in the hills of ancient Greece—at least that is what Lady Mallet called them. She would not have been able to make the comparison if you had stayed for the supper which was quite fine, caviar on toast points and many other delicacies, though served cold when the guests could have used something more warming." Lady Tartte's stomach rumbled beneath the pallid green gown that cleaved tightly to her belly. "I hurried here this morning without taking my own repast."

"Busby, a plate of sweet rolls for Lady Tartte," the duchess called to her butler who lurked nearby. "And now to the point of the matter."

The unwanted guest lowered her voice to the level of intimacy as if they were the best of friends. "Many people spoke of the aggressive behavior of your daughters. The men, of course, whispered of their sylph-like forms in those sheer gowns. Some suggested you did not come inside at Lady Mallet's house out of mortification."

"Angelique was equally sodden! We returned to Bellevue House for dry clothes and a hot meal. Even now, the duke might be coming down with an ague. Lady Mallet planned her frolic far too early in the Season for the well-being of her quests." Outrage made Lady Flora's own perpetually blonde curls quiver.

"Naturally I agree with you, but there is talk that your daughters might be snubbed at upcoming festivities and that Lady Calliope also will be banned from Almack's as the twins are so alike they cannot be trusted not to deceive. Oh, how my heart goes out to you and the duke—and Lord Laughlin. The humiliation!" Lady Tartte clasped her hands to her overflowing bosom, whether from sympathy or in remembrance of James was hard to tell.

The duchess begged to differ. "The Longleighs are never humiliated! In fact, I was about to send my regrets concerning several upcoming occasions as we will be out of town for the next few weeks. Marston and his brother have invited us to visit Castle Blackwater in return for our hospitality. They do not find my daughters inappropriate. I would not be at all surprised if one of them did not return engaged to be Viscountesss Marston."

Busby entered with a tray containing a basket of hot cross buns, the last of the Lenten season, and pots of butter and clotted cream. He set it before Lady Tartte and backed away

"Busby, my spencer, if you please. I find I must be going. Well, just one of these excellent buns before I leave." Lady Tartte stuffed half a roll into her mouth, chewed, swallowed, and washed it down with the tea remaining in her cup. "There, I have regained my strength for the rest of my calls and done my duty to warn you." She rose so swiftly that her green gown dropped another inch lower on her bosom coming treacherously close to exposing her nipples and regaled the duchess with the sight as she made her farewell curtsy. Busby arrived with her wrap and showed her to the door.

"In a hurry to spread the news of our invitation to Blackwater, no doubt," the duchess murmured to herself. "May the mothers of daughters who would snub my girls stew in their envy until nothing is left of them but broth."

Lady Flora returned to the breakfast room to find all the young men vanished and her husband a portrait of congested misery as he attempted to breathe in the steam from a cup of tea. The twins could have posed for portraits of Disappointment and Sorrow as they picked at their food.

"Where are Marston and his brother?" she inquired.

"Gone to say their farewells to the many acquaintances they have made in the city. They seem determined on their country house party no matter what the season and said they would see if others might be interested. Ah-choo!" The duke captured another sneeze in his handkerchief.

"James went with them as they don't know the streets as well as he does. Their first stop is to be Lady Mallet's house," Clio said drearily. "I'd be willing to wager Angelique's mother wants to see Castle Blackwater for herself."

"Yes, and here I'd always thought our family was the most adventurous in England," Callie moped.

"We are! I find I have changed my mind. London is beginning to wear on me already. We will be off to the castle in a matter of days."

Like wilted black-eyed-Susans newly watered, the Longleigh girls perked up immediately. Their breakfast held new appeal, and they called for more buns. After that, their chatter was composed entirely of what they should pack for their visit to Blackwater.

~ * ~

The following morning, Clio and Callie found themselves alone at breakfast. Usually late risers, they'd had trouble staying abed in their excitement over the upcoming trip. Besides, they hadn't gone out to ball or fete or musicale the previous evening as Mama said she wanted them well-rested for the rigors of travel. The young men had gone on the town with James as their guide, however, trying to cram in any missed experiences before leaving London. They'd returned loud and rowdy enough for the entire household to hear. Not surprising that Gareth and Tristan had not yet come down to eat, but strange Mama and Papa were not at the table either.

Since no one stood nearby to hear, they resumed a small argument begun when they lay side by side in the bed and compared their experiences of the last weeks. Clio raised her cup of tea and spoke behind it as if Busby standing in the far corner might read her lips. "But we were to have our first kisses on the same evening!" she said crossly.

"Yet you went into a deserted corridor with Lord Blandon and hid in a curtain," Callie replied.

"He wrapped me in the curtain and had no intension of showering me with tender kisses. He only showed interest in squeezing my bosom and lifting my skirt. When he did that, I was able to draw my stiletto and press it against his side. You've never drawn your knife at all." As if to make her point, Clio fumbled beneath table and drew her weapon from its sheath. She used it to butter her toast before wiping it clean on a napkin and returning it to its place beneath her garment. Busby, silent, kept his eyes averted.

"I've had no need. No one plotted to seduce me. The crush was so bad at Almack's that night, Tristan and I found ourselves caught behind a door as the crowd moved forward when the music began again. That quickly, he laid his lips on mine, so warm and tender, just for a moment. Still, I swear I felt that warmth all the way to the tips of my toes." Callie smiled into her teacup as if it held a fortune foretelling love and happiness.

"Ridiculous. Do you consider yourself engaged to the younger brother now? Perhaps he is only after your dowry," Clio said bitterly.

"Do not try to sully my experience, Clio. He had no time to speak of his feelings or intentions toward me. No one knows of the kiss but Tristan and the two of us." Callie poured a dollop of cream into her tea to cool it and drew her spoon through it to form a heart.

Her sister snorted in a most unladylike way. "Most likely Marston does as well. Maybe that grotesque manservant of theirs also. I am sure they tell each other everything as we do and Oskar might overhear."

"Overhear what? That we love each other?"

The duchess swept into their company and took a seat. "I fear your father is worse and slightly fevered. He is taking only tea, toast and three boiled eggs in his bedchamber this morning."

Before she could go on, the Hardacres joined them, appearing in fine fettle for two young men who has spent the previous night carousing. "I shall truly miss these breakfasts where the food is hot and savory and the company so beautiful," Gareth said, his eyes on Callie, her dusky cheeks reddening.

"But we are glad to learn you will accompany us to Blackwater Castle where we shall still have your beauty to gaze upon even if the porridge grows cold," Tristan said somewhat less eloquently. "Not only *your* pretty faces, of course, but also Lady Angelique's and Miss Downey's as well as their mamas."

"None of them outshine the duchess," Gareth hastened to add. "I did not think Lady Mallet would come until Lady Tartte appeared at her door while we were saying our farewells and informed us of the good news that you had changed your mind, Lady Flora, and lifted our hearts to the highest planes."

"I'm not sure how our father will accommodate everyone, but we shall give up our private chambers and sleep in the great hall like knights of old. We've done it often enough before," Tristan explained while heaping a plate as if he might never have a good meal again.

James entered and made his way to the sideboard, immediately partaking of a large cup of coffee, black. "Ah, that should do it. Gentlemen, I salute your stamina and ability to hold your liquor." He raised his cup in their direction.

"One thing Castle Blackwater has in abundance is strong spirits," Tristan said.

"You learn to handle it early," his brother agreed.

The duchess interrupted this revealing repartee. "James, your father is too ill to travel. I feel I must stay by his side until he is well. A chill killed Pocahontas, you know."

"Oh, no!" Four voices, all of them belonging to twins, said at once.

"Do not say our visit is cancelled," Callie implored, but she gazed at Gareth as she spoke, not at her mother.

"Not if Lady Mallet and her daughter still intend to go, I should say not. James, you will have to stand in for your father and chaperone your sisters."

"But Mama, I have already endur—enjoyed the rustic hospitality of Castle Blackwater, as good port as any in a storm, but I'd thought to return to the continent shortly."

"Recall your promise to me to help bring the girls out into society. A Longleigh never shirks on his word." Lady Flora shook an aristocratic finger at him.

"I've kept my word to assist with the twins. Hell and damnation, I nearly fought a duel for one of them! But now you want me to leave society for—for the Serpent's Mouth." He, too, looked at the food on his plate as if it were a last breakfast.

"Such language! You've always claimed to prefer a wilderness to London during the Season. Now is your opportunity to escape to more rugged surroundings. Finch will go along to tend to the girls, but I am sure Oskar can do for you during this brief stay since you've been sharing your father's valet. The duke will need his man here to fetch and carry while he is ill. I must remain behind to be sure your father does not rise from his bed too soon. Now, I should see if he has eaten all his breakfast, always a good gauge of his health." Considering everything settled, the duchess returned to her husband after ordering her own meal on a tray.

"No need to look so glum, Longleigh, we will have a fine time with the ladies for company," Gareth assured him.

"Ever the optimist, *younger* brother," Tristan said, still playing the heir. I imagine it won't be as amusing to me as London."

Fourteen

The footmen wore out their shoe leather relaying messages between the duchess and Lady Mallet before all details were agreed upon. Reluctantly, Lady Flora conceded that the ducal coach would prove cumbersome on the roads through the marsh and her daughters might be conveyed in Lady Mallet's lighter vehicle. The Baroness Downey had contracted the same ailment as the duke, no doubt spread around like the festive wreaths at the unfortunate frolic. She placed Clarissa in the care of Angelique's mother, thus allowing room for all five ladies in the smaller coach, since at least three of the passengers were slenderly built.

The young men rode astride and Oskar followed with a baggage cart heaped full of the Hardacre's new possessions as well as those of the women. He grumbled to Finch who sat beside him, "I hope the whole blasted top-heavy baggage does not overturn in the swamp and kill us both."

"I am sure your masterful hands will not allow that to happen," she replied, keeping her eyes on the coach some distance ahead.

"Masterful, eh?"

"Yes, quite. Your new eye patch is also very fetching."

"Green satin, matches me livery. Lord Laughlin give it to me out of gratitude when he returned me leather one." Trying to make sure the maid got a good look at it, Oskar took a long stare at Finch, but she continued to gaze straight before her, though her cheeks pinked a bit, perhaps because of the chilly air.

Their party made excellent progress leaving London on the better roads once they'd passed through the usual congested traffic of the city. However, when their vehicles entered the marshes where the paths twisted and twined like writhing water snakes, swift forward progress became nothing but a memory. Lady Mallet's coachman crept along the top of an ancient dike with a drop of three yards lurking on either side waiting to catch an ill-turned wheel and topple the light coach into the murky water.

Clearly, sheep ruled in this domain. If the ewes, many with spring lambs by their sides, took a notion to move from one green, grassy plot to another in the flat landscape, the carriage must wait upon their pleasure until at last the shepherd and his dogs passed like tails wagging behind them. This happened more than once.

The girls wrinkled their noses at the scent of damp wool, but Lady Mallet chided them. "There is wealth in that fleece, and Kentish sheep bring good money when shipped abroad on the hoof. Think of fresh mutton and tender lamb served with mint jelly at the castle far above the stink of the animals and marsh itself. The new marchioness can sit in her airy abode and count her profits." That gave them food for thought and quieted their impatience.

Anxious to show his native land in a good light and make the wait pass more pleasantly, Gareth Hardacre dismounted to converse with the ladies, especially Callie, as yet another herd passed. He leaned in the open door of the carriage and explained, "Romney Marsh sheep are a long wool variety and come in both white and brown colors. They are valued for their ability to fight off foot rot and liver fluke, you know. The sheep keep the grass clipped close and allow it to be dug for sod, another profitable marsh industry."

Angelique's nose twitched again as the breeze brought another whiff of sheep into the carriage, but Clarissa replied, "Interesting."

Searching for a way to engage the twins, Gareth added, "Many think the road we used today was built by the Romans, but actually locals created it during the so-called Dark Ages."

Callie smiled into his eyes, his beautiful blue water eyes, and answered immediately. "As Walpole informed us, it was really an age of chivalry and faith and great achievements."

"With occasional bouts of plague and endless petty wars," Clarissa added. She spoke infrequently but always rather knowingly.

"The Romans would have done a better job of it," James felt moved to say, bending from his saddle. "Ah, the way is clear at last. Forgive me if I dash ahead and outdistance the mosquitoes."

"Our brother hasn't a romantic bone in his body," Clio said, giving one of those snorts her mother so despised as Oskar appeared to give his master a leg up on his mount. He also performed the small service of shutting the carriage door. The coach moved cautiously forward through a mass of sheep droppings.

"I would say Viscount Laughlin is all romance and simply doesn't know it," Angelique offered with a meaningful sigh.

Clio looked out her window, hoping to draw the attention of the supposed Viscount Marston. "Lord Marston is riding beside the baggage cart now. He seems in no hurry to return to his realm."

Angelique slapped away the buzzing insects that had infiltrated the coach while the door stood open. A few pink welts ornamented her upper arms. "No wonder. The place is nothing but a watery maze infested with insects and sheep. Surely he would prefer to spend his time in London if his father would permit it."

"Eyes on the prize, my daughter," Lady Mallet said. "A marchioness outranks all but a duchess, and the other young man has pointed out the sources of their wealth. The mosquitoes will not bother you at the castle. The sea breezes blow them away."

"I'd rather be a duchess," Angelique muttered.

"Don't pin your hopes on James. He means to be gone from England as soon as the Season ends if not before. We've often heard him say he will not marry until he has seen the world and maybe not even then. He has so many brothers, the title is in no danger of going extinct whether he gets an heir or not," Callie told her.

Angelique fanned her hands again. The mosquitoes truly did prefer her plump, white flesh and bothered the little brown girls hardly at all. "The right woman might change his mind."

"I doubt you are she," Clio answered, most likely still peeved at her tactics to get both Marston and her brother as a dancing partner more often than she should.

The carriage turned another bend in the road and Callie called out, "There it is—Castle Blackwater up on the cliff. How perfectly medieval, no recent additions or changes that I can see."

The buildings of a small town, presumably Marston, clustered on the toes of the uplift like small corns and a great bunion on a giant's foot. Those not at work in the fields or on the sea, came to their doors to watch the vehicles pass. Women in aprons with toddlers clinging to their skirts dipped crude curtsies while older sons doffed their caps. Those lingering in the ale house raised their pints at their passage. Painted ladies crowded the open upper windows of a sturdy two-story building with a shining red door and called to the Hardacre twins, "Glad to have you back, laddies. Oooh, I see we have a handsome new visitor, too. Half price for your first visit, lovey."

"What a lovely central window those women have. I should like one similar when I have my own home." Angelique pointed out the scene of sea nymphs lounging on the rocks as they combed the very long hair that covered their most intimate parts, all nicely portrayed in stained glass above the red door. Beneath it, a woman not nearly as pretty but huge of stature and hard of eye glared at their coach from the partly open entrance as it passed.

The Longleigh twins, not as innocent as they should be due to extensive unsupervised reading, snickered. Lady Mallet quickly put down the shades on that side of the carriage. "Do not pay them any mind. They are beneath your notice," she coached her charges.

Their conveyance climbed the steeply inclined path and passed through an open portcullis long rusted into place. Hounds, large and small, spotted or brown or black, raced to meet them and unnerve the horses. A sharp whistle called them back. They milled around the boots of an ill-dressed man, tall, lean, craggy of face and silver of hair, who waded through them to arrive at the carriage door. Gareth wheeled his horse and dismounted, tossing the reins to a groom who hurried forward to take them. James entrusted his thoroughbred to the same man, and pushing dogs aside with his boot tip, went to assist in handing down the ladies.

"Well, well, what have we here?" the older man said, rubbing his hands together like a miser over a chest of gold.

"What we have here are Lady Mallet and her charges. If you are the master of the hounds, please lock them up before they ruin our gowns," replied Angelique's mother, looking down her long and imperious nose at the boorish fellow.

"And here we have Phineas Hardacre, Marquess of Blackwater, in the flesh. The dogs have the run of the place while you do not." He gave her a curt bow that said he outranked her by a long shot, no matter what his appearance. Hair tied back with a black ribbon, it failed to fall across his unshaven face as his sons knew it usually did.

Gareth rushed to make introductions before matters grew worse. "Lady Mallet, her daughter Angelique, the Honorable Clarissa Downey, Lady Clio and Lady Calliope Longleigh, daughters of the Duke of Bellevue. You remember James, Viscount Laughlin, as our former guest." Each young lady made a bob as he ran down the list of names. James merely inclined his head as if to say he'd be a duke one day.

"Aye, I never forget a man who took money off me playing chess. I expect a chance to win it back. Just look at these two, alike as fresh green peas in a pod, but tiny. Doubt either would survive a birthing. The blonde looks likely, but the mosquitoes have been at her, not a good sign that she'll hold up well in the marshes. I'm not altogether sure why you even invited the scrawny one along," Lord Blackwater assessed, not bothering to keep his thoughts to himself.

"Of course, we shall play again. I warn you not to underestimate my sisters. They are actually more like tough dried beans not easily crushed. I am sure the other ladies have hidden merits as well," James drawled, marginally defending the women but not nearly as upset as he should have been by the comments.

"I think we must turn around right this moment and go back to London," Lady Mallet sniffed.

"Excellent idea," James agreed.

"No, we've only just arrived and seen nothing of the castle yet," Clio said with a stamp of her foot.

"Now that one there has some spirit." Lord Blackwater gifted her with a smile that might have been almost pleasant if he hadn't lost a few teeth during his service in the king's navy and done nothing to replace them.

Well-shaven cheeks burning, Gareth rushed to apologize. "Isolation and the lack of gentlewomen in the castle make my father forget his manners. Let's get you inside and see to your chambers for the stay. I am sure Papa has made arrangements for an evening meal. At least, I hope so."

"No one starves at Castle Blackwater. Where is that laggard brother of yours?"

"Coming along with the baggage cart. They should be here shortly."

"He as dandified as you? Is that where my money went? On fine clothes and French barbers?" Lord Blackwater eyed the snug pantaloons, the tight fit of his son's jacket, and the young man's recently shorn hair.

"Let us not forget the Italian shoemaker," James added just to stir the pot.

"We haven't paid for most of it yet, though our monthly tab will soon be due," Gareth confessed.

"Let them come here to collect," his father answered.

At that moment, the baggage cart creaked through the portcullis, drawing the dogs off to investigate the newest arrivals. The pack greeted Oskar with wagging tails and Finch with copious sniffing of her skirts. A few peed on the wheels marking it as their own. Tristan dismounted and called them off. "Back Fido, Blackie, Spot, Rover, and all the rest of you."

"So original, not a Jupiter or Mars or Aphrodite in the bunch," James remarked.

"We cleave to the old ways here, very old ways," their host said as if his words had a deeper meaning. "Since the other boy is here, let's make our way inside. I'll leave the curs in the courtyard because they bother the gentle sensibilities of the ladies," Blackwater said magnanimously and led the way into his domicile.

"A great hall and a castle keep," murmured Callie. "How exciting."

The Hardacre twins exchanged glances as they entered their home. Their father had taken some pains for his anticipated guests. Cobwebs up high were missing from the corners. The slates of the floor possessed the gloss of the recently washed. The huge fireplace meant to heat the entire area had been divested of its blanket of ashes. Even the suits of armor guarding either side of the entry and too small to fit any living Hardacre appeared burnished and free of dust. Three throne-like chairs remained but had been augmented by lesser though similar seating foraged from some attic. Someone had draped the long trestle table in damask and laid out places with jeweled goblets and gold plate that must have been locked away in the strong room for most of its existence. If only Blackwater had taken as much care with his own appearance. His loose garments remained as spotted as some of his dogs, and his boots bore the dust of many days in their creases.

"Ever seen that before?" Tristan whispered to his brother with a nod at the elaborate table setting.

"Never. Mama used china, but of course our father broke most of that when he had his rages."

"Damask, golden plates, and possibly a wicked lord," Clio breathed nearby, close enough for Tristan and Gareth to hear, but not the possibly evil master of Blackwater. "Perfect!"

"Yes, yes, we will dine like royalty tonight, but first show our guests to their chambers in the tower. I offer Lady Mallet here my bed, though I admit I thought a duchess would be honoring us with her presence. The young gals can share the old solar where my boys usually put up." Lord Blackwater had managed to insult the lady's age and rank as well as offer a slightly off-color remark in the same breath.

Liza Mallet's cheeks burned, but she replied coolly. "As I am responsible for Angelique and Clarissa, I'd rather they lodge with me."

"Suit yourself, but it will be three to a bed then, and each of these little sprites will have a mattress to herself. Laughlin, you are at the top of the tower again, the ancient alchemist's chamber, drafty but plenty of bedding. Oskar, show them the way. Oskar?" Blackwater's keen dark eyes scanned the hall.

"Right here, milord."

"Good God, man, what have they done to you in London town? You are tricked out like a Covent Garden whore. Except for your size and that gold earring, I would not have recognized you."

"It's me livery and the wig what fooled ye. I'm dressed like a proper footman now. Where do we put Miss Finch, the ladies' maid?" Oskar asked about the little woman standing in his vast shadow.

"Wherever maids stay. I can't be bothered to think of everything."

"Been many a year since we've had a maid. There's the old housekeeper's chambers off the kitchen. Very snug in there." His one good eye sought to reassure Finch with a wink in her direction.

"Suit yourself, then. Away with all of you! Rest, change your clothes, and do whatever else women need to do before sitting down to supper. Have Cookie send up some wine when you go to settle the maid." Blackwater slumped into one of the throne chairs and contemplated the small fire in the great hearth as if everyone else had ceased to exist.

Oskar escorted the fine ladies to their chambers with James going ahead since he knew the way, then organized a chain of men to haul the boxes from the baggage cart up the twisting staircase illuminated only by a few slits of light from windows narrow as the center of a serpent's eye. He remained on the landing outside the solar while Finch unpacked the girls' belongings into a large standing wardrobe. She was summoned upstairs to do the same task for Lady Mallet, who had expected Lord Blackwater to provide her with a maid only to discover there were none to be had in the castle.

~ * ~

By the time all that was completed, darkness had fallen. Oskar showed Finch to her quarters using a high held lantern. "One thing I learned in London is the gentry can be both wastrels and very cheap all at the same time. I can see how hard ye worked trying to serve them all. In the morning, I'll get some women up from the village to help. Truth be, they don't like to come here, but their curiosity to see high-toned ladies might winkle them out."

"Curiosity is a powerful draw," Finch agreed. "My young ladies have a great deal too much of it, and it has often led them into trouble of the childish variety. They must learn to be more careful now they are out."

Leaving the tower, they entered a steamy kitchen beneath the great hall. The same chimney must have served both fireplaces, but in this subterranean cavern, a more substantial fire crackled as the drippings from two legs of lamb being turned on a spit by a crook-legged dog running in a wheel overflowed a catch pan and hit the flames. A similar animal, equally long-bodied, curly-tailed, mottled, and ugly rested beneath a huge table where a man with the muscles of a pugilist, punched down the dough for the evening bread.

"Ahoy, Bristol, what's for supper?" Oskar greeted the man.

"We butchered a crippled lamb because mutton ain't good enough for the ladies and bread rolls, as you can very well see."

"They'd be used to a soup for a starter and some greens to go with that."

"Would they now? There will be potatoes browned in the grease and carrots. Got some barley and mutton soup from dinner I could heat up, but don't know about any greens."

"Send the kitchen boy down to the village. The lettuces should be up. Fix them with oil and vinegar, salt and pepper. That should do."

"My, ain't we got the fine airs now, and look at you all dressed up like the organ grinder's pet monkey." Bristol crooked a thick pinkie finger in the air. "Been like trying to cook for a bloody admiral all day long. I'll be needing some help if it's to be more than Blackwater and his lads eating."

"I'll see ye get it, mate. And mind the cheddar ain't moldy when you put it out with the nuts."

"Certainly, your lordship." Bristol made a mock obeisance over the lump of dough. He gave it one more punch before twisting off a portion for a roll as if he were wringing the neck of a chicken.

"I believe I would be most comfortable sleeping on a pallet with my young ladies," Finch said with a slight quaver in her voice.

"There, there. See how nice a place I have for ye." Oskar led the way to a door on the other end of the kitchen and opened it with a bow and flourish as if he presented the chamber of a king. A small suite of two rooms revealed itself. Centered in the first area sat a rough table with a brown corked bottle upon it, a chair made to hold a large man beside it, and an ample supply of candles in a box on a shelf nearby. The second chamber held a cot made up with military neatness and covered with a brown woolen blanket. Large, mucky boots still sat at its foot, and wall pegs held clothes worn hard and due for a washing. Self-consciously, Oskar ripped them down and bundled the garments in his arms. Fortunately, the smell of roasting lamb covered their sour odor.

"This is your chamber," Finch remarked. "I could not think of taking it. Besides, I am not so very sure about sharing space with Mr. Bristol and the two hounds."

"Oh, Bristol has a woman in the village. He goes there once the evening meal is finished and the kitchen boy has washed up. As for the turnspit dogs, they make good company and keep your feet warm on a cold night. Ollie and Ottie they're called. Give them a scrap and a scratch of the belly, and they're your friends for life. They'll sound the alarm, too, if a stranger enters the kitchen. I'll be sleeping right here on a pallet before your door to keep you safe."

"Why Oskar, how chivalrous of you."

Oskar stared down at the toes of the best shoes he'd ever worn, a newborn habit he couldn't seem to shake in her presence. "No, Miss Finch. You showed me some kindnesses in London, mending me livery and showing me how to act and such. There be rough men who come here. In fact, I am one of them, but you need not fear the others while I am about."

"What of my girls? Are they safe?"

"I believe me boys will keep them so, and Lord Laughlin seems doughty enough and handy with weapons. Still, one never knows with Blackwater and the doings in the Serpent's Mouth."

Oskar left her to unpack her own meager belongings. Not reassured by his words, Finch opened her small trunk and hung up her spare gown and her Sunday garment where Oskar's clothes once held place.

Fifteen

Blackwater, mellowed by the two goblets of red wine Oskar, still dressed in his ridiculous finery served to the Marquess, proved to be a convivial host, at least for this first evening in the castle. He told them tales of his time serving under the deeply lamented Admiral Lord Nelson.

"My own father sent me to sea at the age of twelve. No need for the spare to linger about the castle when he should be out making his way in the world. Both the best and worst years of my life. I would have done the same with Tristan, but Gareth vowed he'd run away to sea also if I parted them. Had to show them who was master of the household once my brother shoved off this mortal coil and I got called home to take his place. I put up with none of their switches and pranks. But the younger boy took ill, and my wife did naught but cry, so he stayed."

Blackwater stretched out his goblet for a refill from one of the two ewers Oskar held. The second contained well-watered wine for the ladies. Lady Mallet summoned him to renew her own cup. "I believe that phrase is 'shuffled off this mortal coil' from *Hamlet* written by the immortal bard."

"How would I know? My brother went to university. I went to sea and got the better education in how to go on in life. Look at him drowning after living all his life by the sea but rarely going into it. Feared the surf, he did, while I helped strip the wrecks that ran aground from an early age. Home on leave from the navy, I plucked the greatest prize from the ocean. You've seen her portrait in the solar, the last marchioness and a beauty. My brother had that painted hoping to make her his if I died in one of Nelson's reckless maneuvers. He desired her."

Blackwater leaned heavily toward Lady Mallet seated on his right and breathed in her face. She drew back. "Yes, I noted the painting. She is shown with a ewe and lamb at her feet and the castle and marshes in the background, very much the lady of the manor, so I suspect you might be right. Her sons certainly inherited those striking blue eyes and rich, dark hair."

"Pulled her from the ocean by those tresses thick as seaweed. She owed me her life, and I took her..." The marquess' black-eyed glance roved the length of the table and scanned the wide eyes and open mouths of the younger ladies. "...to the priest and married her at once. The twins came along nine months later, but I'd returned to sea by then. My brother had the raising of them and spoiled the boys before I came home to take his place." Blackwater leaned back in his seat again and shot his goblet out for more wine.

Oskar nodded urgently to the kitchen boy to bring in the platter of roasted lamb and vegetables. Almost creating a miracle, Cookie had served up barley soup in the remaining chipped porcelain bowls and followed it with a poached sole swimming in a white sauce that covered its dull blue eyes. No salad appeared, but its lack was not too noticeable with the carrots and potatoes surrounding the haunch. Blackwater stood a trifle unsteadily to carve and portion out the meat as Oskar brought the mismatched china plates, some willow pattern, some French Sevres, to him for filling. Evidently, the gold chargers had been unearthed merely for show, though the jeweled goblets were put to immediate use.

Wielding the carving knife more like a saber as he hacked the meat from the bone, Blackwater completed his task and slumped back into his carved chair. He tucked into a rare slice cut from near the center and filled the rest of his mouth with potato. Swallowing, he felt moved to continue his tale.

"I believe my wife was a witch, a witch from the sea, as she did not drown like any other woman would have. She cast her spell upon me and my brother both. Her blood was Irish, and who can trust them? I stayed ashore long enough to be certain of her condition, then allowed her to write home about her great luck in surviving the wreck and claiming so fine a husband as myself." Blackwater removed a bit of carrot from his teeth with the tine of his fork and pointed the prongs towards his guests. "She wanted the heir just as all of you do."

The girls quailed beneath his vicious stare. James, seated on the marquess' other side, merely raised his brows. "My sisters are great heiresses and actually can choose to marry whomever they wish. The others have adequate dowries. None of them need covet Castle Blackwater."

"The castle has its own power, Laughlin. Perhaps my wife, when she saw the sea could not kill me, ensorcelled my brother to go into the waves and die so she might command it."

Gareth shoved back his throne-like chair and stood. "Our mother did no such thing!"

"I returned home to find her working in the alchemist's chamber with herbs and potions."

"She sought a cure for the marsh fever and tried local remedies. Only the Jesuit bark allayed her chills and sweats, but in the end even that did not help."

By his side as always, Tristan stretched out a hand. He no longer wore the red ribbon on his person, nor did Gareth bear the blue. They had resumed their lots in life without a word to any others. "Sit, brother. We know the truth. In the end, she had no will to live. If our father does not own it, then so be it. We invited these ladies here to choose our brides if they will have one or both of us. Our fate rests in their hands."

Lord Blackwater slapped the table and cackled. "Spoken like some ninny from one of Mrs. Radcliffe's novels. Oskar, bring on the cheese and more wine! After we finish, perhaps these fine examples of womanhood will display their musical accomplishments for our amusement."

Lady Mallet jostled Angelique lightly with her elbow. It seemed almost an accident, but the girl got the point. "Why yes, I play the pianoforte and adore singing. I would be pleased to perform for you."

"We shall do one of our duets," Clio replied immediately, not about to be upstaged.

"I also play the pianoforte," Clarissa, who had been largely silent throughout the meal, said.

"They all do—with greatly varying amounts of ability," James drawled.

"Very good, but I don't possess such an instrument. They must sing without accompaniment up there in the minstrel's gallery." Blackwater pointed to a balcony overlooking the hall, an opening they had passed on the way to their chambers.

"I can play the harp," Clarissa added, peering hard around the great hall as if such a large instrument might be sitting unnoticed in one of the dark corners unlit by the branches of candles on the table and the flickering firelight.

"My late wife played a small Irish harp, always singing dolorous songs the way those people do. It might still be in the casket up there if you want to give it a try. It's been many a year since we've had music here. In fact, why not begin now while the gentlemen enjoy their port. I have no withdrawing room, you see." The lord of the manor waved the candidates for the next marchioness toward the stairs. After a moment's hesitation, Lady Mallet nodded. James Longleigh merely chuckled as they filed away to reappear on the small gallery.

Clarissa Downey immediately opened the lid of a heavy chest and drew out a lap harp. She turned the tuning pegs and was rewarded with a plink as one of the rotted strings broke. "This won't do. Ah, I think I see a recorder." She unearthed the long wooden tube, blew off the dust, and set her mouth to the top of the instrument. Fingering a few notes, she nodded. "This will work to accompany the singing if the songs are simple."

"I would never allow Angelique to play such a vulgar instrument. It distorts the face and purses the mouth in an unladylike way," Lady Mallet proclaimed.

"It is from the days of old and very fitting, I think, for music in a castle" Callie said. "Do you know *The Turban'd Turk?*" She delved into the box and withdrew a pair of tambourines with tarnished brass jingles rimming their edges. Handing one to her sister, she whispered, "As we rehearsed for Lady Mallet's frolic."

"Make it lively!" Blackwater shouted at them from below as if they were hired minstrels earning their bread and butter.

Mortification kept the Hardacre twins silent, but James laughed again. "I suspect this will be more interesting than most musicales I've been forced to attend."

Clarissa began puffing into the recorder, her legs slightly splayed and her long fingers spidering up and down the holes in the shaft. The twins rattled their tambourines to the refrain, *dum-dum-a-dimmy, dum-a-dum* twice repeated and accented by a bounce off their hips of the instruments on each *dum*. Clio sang the first verse in a sweet and merry voice.

> *Hey! A turbaned Turk who scorns the world*
> *May strut about with his whiskers curled*
> *Keep a hundred wives under lock and key*
> *For nobody else but himself to see*
> *Yet long must he pray with his Al Koran*
> *Before he can love like an Irishman*

On the chorus, the sisters danced around each other, paused, and allowed Callie to take up the second verse claiming no other race could love like an Irishman. Englishmen had an entire verse to their honor but it ended with *And I know she'll say from behind her fan/ Nobody loves like an Irishman.* Callie sang the last verse extolling Irish lovers and both repeated the chorus three times to bring the song to its end.

Below them, Lord Blackwater joined in and even Oskar standing in a dim corner clapped along and thumped a large foot in time to the tambourines. All of the men applauded with enthusiasm, Lady Mallet only politely.

"Now that's a fine ditty if I've ever heard one. I would not mind hearing those sweet voices for years on end," Blackwater declared.

"Angelique, quickly, your *Robin Adair*," Lady Mallet prompted.

Angelique moved forward to supplant the twins. "*Robin Adair* by Lady Caroline Keppel—which I shall sing a cappella." She nodded toward Clarissa, red-faced from blowing into the recorder, to desist in her efforts. Knotting her hands in front of her, she sang the more sentimental song in a high soprano along with a creditable Scottish lilt to her voice.

Blackwater applauded with less enthusiasm at its finish. "Very good but not spirited enough for my tastes. What else can you offer, my comely blonde Miss?"

Lady Mallet cleared her throat of outrage before she spoke. "I believe my charges are in need of rest after their long journey. If your man will light our way, we should adjourn to our sleeping chambers for the night."

"All right then. Oskar, lead them away. You, Laughlin, you'll stay for a game of chess."

Whether an order or a suggestion, James agreed and bid good-night to his sisters.

Sixteen

"But we aren't tired, are we, Callie? I feel as if I could stay up until dawn," Clio argued as Finch, replete from an enormous meal of every delicacy the girls had dined upon and furnished by Oskar, helped them into their nightdresses.

"Please, Lady Clio, do not give me any trouble. I can barely keep my eyes open, and I must still go upstairs and assist the other ladies before I can seek my own bed."

"Thoughtless of us," said Callie as she perched on the side of one of the identical tester beds in the room and wondered which Hardacre twin usually slept there, the heir or her spare.

Clio spun around in her modest and plain white gown revealing her slippers of bright red wool. A shawl of the same color and knit by the same source, her mother, belled out like a cape from her shoulders. James had warned them the castle was plagued by unpleasant drafts, and Finch had packed accordingly. Blue slippers peeped from beneath Callie's nightdress. True, the floor was cold, but a brazier filled with coals heated the air of the chamber. Tall wrought iron holders bore the weight of candles so thick and heavy they might burn for a year and a day and provided enough light for a small chapel

Finch settled a cap edged in lace on each dark head. "Better safe than sorry. We wouldn't want a congestion to settle in your brain."

"It's perfectly warm and wonderfully eerie with all the cast shadows. I do believe the ghost of the late marchioness might step down from her portrait and play us a tune on her harp," Clio insisted.

The woman in the painting did clutch her favorite instrument as if she strummed her long fingers across the strings. At that moment, the wind hummed through the thin cracks in the old wooden shutters that covered the sole window. All three of them startled, then laughed, the wind of course, only the wind.

Callie retrieved an object she'd hidden beneath her pillow. "Do see, I've brought Mama's copy of *The Castle of Otronto* from the library at Bellevue Hall. We could read it aloud to each other in this perfect setting. We should invite the other girls to join us. Finch, will you convey our message?"

"Certainly, my dear young ladies, but they may not have your stamina. Some might want their rest."

"You are dismissed for the night once you have finished with them. We can certainly tuck ourselves in now that we are grown, dear Finch." Clio waved her toward the door.

"I still feel uneasy about leaving you in this place alone," the maid said as she left.

"Ah, but twins are never alone. We will be fine. The shutters have so many gaps, if we cried out, James would hear us." Callie reassured herself by saying so.

To their surprise, light footsteps sounded on the stone steps not long after. Angelique and Clarissa had helped each other change. Only Lady Mallet held out for Finch's services. Her hair swathed in an enormous mobcap tied beneath her chin, Liza Mallet appeared in a dressing gown of oriental splendor and curly-toed slippers. She seated herself in the only chair placed closest to the brazier. Patting her head, she announced, "Who knows when my hair will be properly dressed again in this barbarous place? I must preserve what I can of my coiffure, and I'd advise you to do the same."

"Oh, Finch fixes hair quite well," Callie assured her.

"Certainly not as well as my London hairdresser so many miles away. I understand we are here for a reading of Walpole's gothic novel. Proper setting, I must say. Girls, under the covers before you catch a chill."

The two girls piled into one of the beds and drew the covers up. The twins did the same in the other bed after carefully positioning the candles to provide light for the reading but still a safe distance from the bed hangings.

Opening the slim volume bound in suede and stamped in gold, Callie began. "*The Castle of Otronto* by Horace Walpole. *For the glorious Duchess of Bellevue, Lady Flora Longleigh, the finest of fair ladies and a rare blossom among women. Your devoted, Horace.* Oh! I had no idea Mama knew him so very well. I wonder what Papa thought of this?"

Lady Mallet waved her hand as if brushing away one of the swamp's mosquitoes. "Disregard. Horace was a terrible flirt and only pursued women he knew he could never attain, your mother among them. He had no real interest in the female sex or in marriage and never took a bride."

"How strange when he had a title to pass along," Angelique said, stifling a yawn by placing a hand over her pretty pink lips.

The twins, however, exchanged knowing glances as if they'd listened into conversations they weren't meant to hear fairly often. Clarissa sighed, saying straight out, "Oh for heaven sakes, he preferred the company of men in all ways."

"I still don't understand."

"Later, after you are married, I will explain all," Angelique's mother told her. "Read on."

"Shall I skip the two prefaces?"

"Please, please do." The group was unanimous in that. "You realize most of Walpole's friends regarded the story as a jest, and he felt it necessary to justify his work with explanations afterwards," Lady Mallet informed them, further delaying the reading.

"Thank you for that insight," Callie said with a hint of irritation. "I shall begin again."

Manfred, Prince of Otronto, had one son and one daughter; the latter, a most beautiful virgin, aged eighteen, was called Matilda.

She read past the crushing of the Manfred's son by a giant helmet that fell from the sky and the arrest of a handsome and well-spoken peasant lad for the crime. The young man was duly imprisoned beneath the helm once the body of the crushed heir had been removed. Clio took over for her favorite passage where the evil prince attempts to seduce his son's intended, the Princess Isabella, to get another son, even though still married to the saintly Hippolita. She added great drama by portraying Isabella's voice as high and quavering and Manfred's as gruff and lascivious. Clearly the only one who had never read the story before, Angelique listened avidly as Isabella fled to a subterranean chamber to escape his advances.

Placing a pair of gold-rimmed spectacles drawn from her sleeve on her nose, Clarissa took the book to continue the reading. The other girls stared at her. "Your vision is poor, Clary?" Callie asked.

"Very nearsighted, I'm afraid, though my far sight is better. Mama will not allow me to wear them in public. She says no man wants a woman with weak eyesight lest she pass that along to his sons. I stumble and bumble about Almack's trying to find a husband so I can wear my spectacles at last. Truthfully, I'd rather be a Bluestocking than be married off for my modest dowry, as it certainly shan't be for my beauty."

"Perhaps someone will marry you out of true love," said Callie. Clio snorted.

"I would settle for a man who enjoys my company and might allow me to pursue my intellectual interests."

"You have no expectations of marrying one of the Hardacres, then?" Angelique probed.

Clarissa laughed in a pleasantly warm tone. "I suspect I am here simply to fill a minor role like the comic servants in this book. Those twins have no interest in me. Only Mama continues to hope."

"Could we get back to the story then? I find it thrilling," Angelique prompted.

Clarissa read on. Lady Mallet sunk into a doze during one of the long and windy passages. Her head nodded and her aristocratic nose issued a whistling noise at every exhale. The girls ignored it just as they did the wind forcing its fingers through the cracks in the shutters. About the time the gibbering servants reported a giant foot appearing in the Castle of Otronto, James passed on the staircase. He issued an impertinent knock on their door.

"I say, lamps out in there, or do you plan to chatter all night."

"Go away. We will read as long as we wish," Clio answered with equal impertinence.

"Improving your mind, are you?" Still, her brother continued on his way to the alchemist's chamber, laughing as he went.

Unfortunately, his loud rap awakened Lady Mallet momentarily. "What, what was that noise? Is someone attempting to break in? Call the footmen!"

"Never fear, only James trying to order us about. Angelique, your turn." Callie gestured for the book to be turned over.

Angelique, not the best of readers but certainly the most enthusiastic, punctuated every exciting passage with gasps or squeaks of dismay or deep sighs, especially when Matilda fell in love with a young man, sight unseen, by listening to the sound of his voice beneath her window. However, when Manfred returned to rant and issue more mad threats, first Lady Mallet nodded off, then Clarissa with her spectacles still on her nose. Angelique stopped reading in mid-sentence and dropped off into the sweet oblivion of sleep with the book open upon her lap. Callie wiggled from the warmth of the covers and retrieved her mother's volume, stowing it carefully under her pillow.

Clio removed the glasses from Clarissa's nose and set them on a small table to prevent their being broken. "I suppose that is all of *The Castle* we are going to read tonight. We can continue tomorrow evening as I hardly think we will have any balls to attend.

"True. If there were, we'd be expected to provide the orchestra most likely."

The girls crawled under the blankets again and arranged themselves back to back much in the same position they'd occupied in Lady Flora's womb. They soon slept, breathing softly against their pillows.

Seventeen

A greater draft than the one seeping through the cracks in the wooden shutters filled the room as one of the dusty and tattered tapestries depicting a unicorn being embraced by a virgin in a flowery garden belled outward. Reluctant to enter, Gareth and Tristan Hardacre peered from behind it.

"We cannot do it tonight with all of them clustered together like so many hens in a coop, no matter what the old man says. We should never do it at all." Gareth shut the hidden door and gestured for Tristan to precede him down the narrow stairs and light the way.

"He will keep insisting, but I agree. If Lady Mallet awoke and started shrieking, Laughlin would come running with a sword in one hand and pistol in the other. He may enjoy mocking his sisters, but his honor would never allow them to come to harm. I also suspect he'd shoot first before waiting to see who molested the women."

Though the staircase continued downward, they emerged from behind another arras depicting knights on chargers that gave them access to the great hall where their father still sat brooding over the chessboard. "Won again, that rascal, and my good coin in his pocket," Blackwater muttered. "Back so soon. You have no stamina. I pity the lassies with you for their husbands. Soft like my brother, soft like your mother, most probably soft in other ways. In my day, I could go at it all night and the woman knew she'd been taken four times over."

"We will not rape them. We will persuade them to marry us," Gareth insisted.

"What, with pretty words? You heard their brother. Those twins are great heiresses and can have whom they please. The mighty Duke of Bellevue would never give his consent for them to accept the likes of you two. He ain't likely to be impressed by a crumbling castle and water meadows full of sheep. Too bad we can't reveal our other enterprises. Take their maidenheads like I told you and that settles it."

Tristan scowled like a man with a long-held grudge. "There are other considerations I tried to tell you. While in London, Gary and I switched places. Clio has her heart set on the heir and took to me unknowing."

"Up to your old tricks. She never saw you naked then."

"Certainly not! I must tell her my true status first before we…"

"Fool! Show her the mark after you take her and let her weep. Your mother wasn't so keen on wedding a second son either, but I gave her no choice. Relieved her of her virginity before I dragged her to the priest. That settled the matter, but I took note not to scare off those little lambs with the truth before you lead them to the slaughter."

Grimacing at his father's crudeness, Gareth sat and leaned across the vacant chessboard. "There are other complications. All of the women were gathered in one place tonight. We could not lure two away without rousing the others. Laughlin would hear any screams and come running. We might both die."

Blackwater rubbed a chin sprouting a silver evening stubble. "In that case, I'd take the blonde for myself and get another heir. A problem solved." The idea amused him so much his laughter filled the great hall and echoed in the stairwells. Spittle foamed in the corners of his mouth and he wiped it away with a less than clean handkerchief.

"I see you can't manage without my help. I'll order Oskar to make sure all of them are locked into their places tomorrow night, including Laughlin. He must cheat at chess though I always watch him carefully. How I will enjoy snatching his sisters out from under his highly superior nose."

"Might be Laughlin simply plays better than you," Tristan answered. "Only Gary has defeated him. As for locking him away, I would not underestimate him."

"No, he must cheat because I am the master planner. You say you prefer these twins above all others, and I'll admit the very idea of them is fetching, so do as I tell you. Take them down to the dungeon where none can hear their screams and have at them. I hold the priest's living. He'll have you married in no time. I'm oh so sorry if one of them doesn't get to marry an heir—unless you'd like me to have either. Then, one could be marchioness now and the other later. The idea appeals even more than taking the blonde girl, in case she should turn out to be as high in the instep as her mother. That sort is never good at bed sports. Now, those twins are saucy, and you say the mother birthed ten alive. That's sporting blood in their veins."

He might have been far gone in his cups, but Blackwater took note of the disgust on the faces of his sons. "Prissy little misses, you are, too. Help an old man get to his nest for the night."

Obeying, his sons hoisted him from his seat and moved their father toward a thick pallet by the fire. "No, no, got to piss first." Fumbling with his buttons, Blackwater opened his flap and poured a long stream into the dying fire. The odor of steaming urine filled the air. Without bothering to rebutton, he fell back into the bed Oskar had prepared for him, since all the chambers held guests.

"Like the knights of old, we sleep in the great hall tonight, my sons. Like knights of old. How does that bastard beat me at chess?"

"You might drink less before taking him on again," Gareth suggested, but his words were wasted on the wastrel. Blackwater had passed out.

The young men prepared more carefully for bed, stripping down to their shirts and folding their clothes carefully before taking to their pallets placed close together and a distance from their snoring father. Gareth, hands folded behind his head, stared up at the distant ceiling.

"What shall we do? How can we tell our beloveds of our deceit?"

"I imagine Lady Calliope will be elated to find out you are the heir. As for me, revealing my status will be a true test as to whether Clio loves me or my supposed title more."

Gareth's fist whipped out and punched his brother in the arm. "Do not speak of Callie as if she were after nothing but a fortune and a title. She constantly assures me she finds primogeniture unfair and insists a man must be judged by his own merits."

Tristan cuffed his brother's ear. "Then she hasn't a practical bone in her tiny body. The law is the law and cannot be changed. I am about to lose the most enticing woman I have ever met because of an accident of birth."

"Do not disparage the woman I adore."

Gareth launched himself from his pallet to land atop his brother and got in a good swipe before Tristan rolled over onto the floor, gained the upper hand, and returned the blow. Twined like a double-headed serpent, they traversed the flags, one on top, now the other, until two huge hands grabbed their shirts and separated them. Oskar shook them like two pups he held by the scruff.

"None of this. Ye haven't fought so since ye were lads. It's over the young ladies, ain't it? Which ye shall have, no?"

"No! We know which we want, but Tristan spoke ill of Lady Calliope. I won't have it!"

"Now, she's a sweet girl, Tris. Apologize to your brother."

"Sorry. I anticipated my own disappointment and took it out on you. May you be happy with your bride."

Oskar nodded his approval. "There you go. Accept, Gareth."

"Apology accepted."

"I know for sure the twins favor you. All will be well, and before long the castle will have a lovely young mistress and mayhap even a competent housekeeper. Wouldn't that be fine?"

"If fairy tales come true," Tristan muttered.

"Back to your beds now. I have another place to be."

The Hardacre twins returned to their pallets and settled again for the night. Lord Blackwater smiled, scheming even in his drunken stupor.

Eighteen

Callie opened the worn wooden shutter and let in the same brisk breeze that had striped the sun of her fragile veils of morning fog and left her naked and ravished for all to see. Clio, her dark, curly head barely peeking from the covers, groaned and pleaded, "Please close that window!"

"It is going to be a beautiful day, a special day, I can tell," her twin retorted.

Still in her chair, Lady Mallet awoke and stretched. "I believe I have crick in my neck, possibly permanent. How I wish I'd brought my own maid to work out the knot." She patted her huge mob cap. "At least my coiffure has been preserved. Where is that girl of yours? I shall need assistance with my attire."

Looking much like an owl that had been disturbed in its roost, Clarissa sat up in bed and groped for her spectacles. Clio slipped from the covers and handed them to her. Beside Clarissa, Angelique slept on with her golden curls arrayed across the pillow like the Sleeping Beauty of the fairy tales. Her mother shook her shoulders. "Up, up, slugabed! We must prepare for another day in this wretched place." With that urging, she marshaled her wards and marched them out the door and up the steps to their own accommodations.

Finch arrived shortly thereafter and took care of her own ladies before answering the incessant demands of Lady Mallet to attend her at once. "There now, don't you both look charming in your sprigged muslins? Do remember your bonnets and wraps if you step outside today. Breakfast has been laid out on the table in the Great Hall and is substantial if not delicate. Keep your eyes only on the food. Ignore the rest as if unseen."

Puzzled, the twins made their way downward. They chattered about what plans might be made for the day: a day on the beach, an exploration of a tower spotted across the inlet from their window, a visit to a herd to pet wooly lambs. The trestle table held a vat of porridge dotted with butter pats and large enough to feed the crew of a frigate. Beside it sat a pot of honey and a cask of raisins. A lovely porcelain bowl offered lumps of sugar and a matching pitcher some cream. Tea and coffeepots sat at the ready. To give the cook credit, he had provided platters of crisply fried kippers and rashers of bacon. They had certainly eaten worse at their many boarding schools which always seemed to have an egg-only-on-Sundays rule, or perhaps one for good behavior which the twins never received.

As they filled their bowls and drizzled the porridge with honey, they could not help but let their eyes stray to the bundle of blankets upon a pallet before the fire. It stirred, and the Marquess of Blackwater emerged like a hatching reptile wriggling from its rubbery shell. Apparently, he had slept in all his clothes, something to be thankful for, though his flap hung open. The twins averted their eyes and dropped the lord of the manor a curtsy he did not see as he turned away to button his britches. "Good morning," they piped.

"Is it? We shall see." Blackwater raked his hands through his grizzled hair, pulling some from his queue. He kicked the bedding aside and stalked toward the door leading to the kitchen. "Such shrill little voices you have so early in the day," he commented before descending into Cookie's realm. A puff of steam escaped as he vanished.

Clio and Callie eyed each other and burst into laughter. Two other rolls of bedding tidily folded sat against the wall, but their occupants had long been gone. The Hardacre twins reappeared now as if they'd ridden in on the mist from the kitchen. Their cheeks were freshly shaved, their clothes neatly arrayed. They held out their hands and the girls went to them, each knowing the one she preferred without asking by some minute revelation of stance or glance.

"If you would prefer something else to eat, simply ask for it," Tristan said, gazing into Clio's eyes as their fingers touched.

"Anything, anything at all if it is in our power to provide," Gareth echoed as he pressed Callie's hand to his lips.

"Obviously, you were never sent away to school. We have eaten our share of porridge," Callie said with a smile. He still retained her hand warm in his.

"No, we were tutored here by men far superior in manners than our father, but we, too, have eaten a quantity of porridge."

Fortunately, Lady Mallet could be heard coming from a distance in the echoing staircases and high-vaulted chambers. Gareth dropped her hand, and Tristan was quick to follow his example.

"Who knows what horrors we shall have to endure today?" Lady Mallet made her grand entrance with her entourage coming behind and followed by Finch, frazzled from waiting on so many. She surveyed the offerings on the trestle table. "What? No eggs, no toast, no marmalade? Never let it be said I am too particular, but really, porridge. Porridge is for infants and peasants."

"Our apologies, Lady Mallet. I am sure Cookie can provide toast and has a pot of jam somewhere," Gareth told her like the heir in full command, but graciously. "Oskar, would you see to that?"

Oskar had emerged from the kitchen in the wake of his masters and quickly rolled up the marquess' scattered bedding. He'd set aside his wig and livery and wore the plain clothes from the hooks in his room below stairs. A faint aroma of the turnspit dogs who had kept him company on his pallet last evening anointed him and made Angelique wrinkle her nose as he passed nearby. "I will, milord. Miss Finch could help me, perhaps."

"I'd be happy to," Finch said, scuttling toward the kitchen as if trying to escape Lady Mallet and her demands.

The twin girls, spooning their porridge at the far end of the table, heard him whisper to their maid, "And for you especially, I will find an egg." The girls exchanged glances, small smiles, and a murmured confidence. "We are not the only ones in love."

After seeing Lady Mallet settled as far away as possible with a cup of coffee christened with a large lump of sugar, Tristan and Gareth came to sit with them. "What is your pleasure for the day?"

"Oh," said Callie. "Could we explore the ancient tower across the way?"

"Not ancient, I fear. It is a Martello Tower built recently to ward off Napoleon's invasion and filled to the brim with redcoats," Tristan told her.

Angelique moved farther from her mother and closer to them, bringing her bowl with her, while Lady Mallet bore down on a plate of kippers. "Truly? The officers are so dashing."

"And only looking to marry a foolish young lady with a decent dowry so they can retire in luxury, the lot of them," her mother supplied.

"Still, it is an interesting structure, and I would like to see it," Clarissa said.

"That settles it. We shall visit the Martello Tower after breakfast."

"Ah, but I so wanted to walk on the beach," Clio pouted.

Tristan assured her, "We have time for both. I'll ask for a picnic basket, and we will dine on the shingle."

James had entered sometime during this discussion. "The tower with its swiveling gun saved the ship I arrived on from the French." He ignored the porridge and filled a plate with bacon and kippers. As Oskar returned with his large hands full with a plate and jam pot, he snatched two pieces of toast before it could be set down in front of Lady Mallet. The bread appeared slightly burnt on one side and untoasted on the other, but he spread it with butter and ate it anyway. Lady Mallet examined the offering that remained, turned up her nose, and shoved her portion in his direction.

"Do sit here by me and tell the tale," she encouraged him, making a discreet motion for Angelique to move closer.

"Leave that to me," a gruff voice said. Lord Blackwater, shaved patchily like a man out of practice but wearing fresh clothes, seated himself between Lady Mallet and Angelique, who edged away again. Clarissa sat next to James across the table eager to hear his tale and not too proud to show that she enjoyed a good bowl of porridge, especially with a generous amount of raisins thrown into the mix.

"What you might not know, Laughlin, is that your father, the mighty Duke of Bellevue, came begging to my castle door to get my permission to build the tower on my land. I allowed it and saved the life of his heir when that French privateer chased your ship into the Serpent's Mouth. The gun holed the mast and sent the Frogs running. Then we led you from the surf, saved your hide. Good thing I have a crew of men experienced in salvaging wrecks."

James raised an eyebrow and applied a layer of strawberry jam to his bread. "I recall Oskar taking me from the surf and must thank my father for his foresight when next I see him. I have thanked you for your hospitality and returned it by inviting your sons to London. Now, we return to Castle Blackwater with the slight possibility that our families might be united. I believe I have been grateful enough."

For a moment, the great hall fell silent. Then Blackwater laughed with head thrown back. "You arrogant bastard. Damned if we won't claim one of your sisters, if not both."

Offended at this language, Lady Mallet stood, forcing everyone else at the table to rise. "Ladies, we shall adjourn to our chambers until time for our excursion to the tower. You, Oskar, have Finch bring me my breakfast on a tray. I require a boiled egg and properly toasted bread."

She swept from the room and drew the other ladies with her as if she had thrown that lifeline into the surf and saved their very lives.

~ * ~

The women waded through the dogs milling in the courtyard with Callie pausing to pat some eager heads and crowded into the light carriage for the trip to the tower. The men elected to ride and a few of the hounds decided to accompany them. Their company, sighted by the man on watch atop the tower, was greeted with enthusiasm by four-and-twenty extremely bored soldiers and their commanding officer, Captain Digby Thornton.

"So pleased you have graced us with your presence on this side of the cove, Lord Blackwater." The captain, a fairly handsome young man with well-groomed side whiskers framing a heavy jaw and calculating dark eyes cast toward the ladies, bowed and scraped.

Blackwater did the honors, introducing them all. "Not much action here since we saved this one from the privateer." He jerked his head in James' direction.

"Oh, we keep busy, run the canon about and shoot a few balls into the sea for practice. One must be ready for Napoleon's invasion. We hear rumors he will come in through Kent."

"Be at ease, sir. I have it on good authority that Boney has given up all thoughts of taking England and turns instead to the rest of Europe," James assured him. He left out that his sister, Iris and her husband had spied out this very information but would never be given public credit for their efforts.

Rather than being reassured, the captain's mighty jaw tightened as if he wanted to crack walnuts with his teeth. "Then, why do we linger here on the edge of a swamp? How is a man to rise in ranks if there is no battle to show his mettle? Who will notice my promise as an officer?" Again, his eyes roved to the cluster of ladies.

"Captain, I believe Great Britain is always at war somewhere in the world. Your chance will come."

Thornton let go of his clench and offered a smile. "Of course. Until then, I will remain vigilant. Allow me to show our beauteous company my small command." He took great care to offer his arm to assist Lady Mallet in crossing a rather flimsy bridge laid over a dry moat to the second story of the tower. "When—if the attack comes, we simply draw in the bridge to deter the enemy," he explained.

Calling the men to attention at the foot of their neatly made up cots which circled the room, he repeated the introductions. The fellow had such a keen ear for ranks and titles, he got not a single one wrong. "Now who will climb up and see my mighty cannon? It is a heavy artillery piece with a swivel of three-hundred sixty degrees. We shall perform a drill for you." He called out orders and sent his men running. James rolled his eyes, but the girls appeared delighted at the prospect.

After getting all the women up to the top of the tower where the stiff breeze molded their gowns close to their limbs and attempted to snatch away bonnets too casually tied, the common soldiers ran their sole cannon around the rim and aimed it out to sea. Lady Mallet planted a hand firmly on top of her large chapeau bearing two plumes that spread out like gulls wings ready to fly.

"Cover your ears against the blast, ladies," the captain prompted. With amazing speed, the redcoats readied the cannon and fired it into the ocean, making a very substantial splash. Startled, Lady Mallet raised her hand and her bonnet took to the air only to be saved by a quick snatch of the hand by James.

"And that is how we drove off the privateer and saved the life of Lord Laughlin," said the captain, oblivious to the damage he had caused to the ladies' garments.

Unaware at first that the gusts had carried a great deal of smut backward and peppered their white gowns, the girls squealed with delight. Angelique removed her hands from her ears and raised both palms to her cheeks. "How thrilling!" She left behind black imprints of her fingertips on her fair skin.

"With your permission, Lady Angelique." Captain Thornton removed the marks with a plain white handkerchief and this time left behind a pair of blushing cheeks.

"So gallant!"

Clarissa removed the spectacles she had defiantly worn and cleaned them with her own embroidered hankie. She wiped her face with the same and turned to inspect the drainage system of the tower. "Does it supply a cistern?"

"Indeed, it does in the base of the tower. Grey," he said to a subordinate. "Take the young lady to see our stores."

A strapping, gray-eyed young man who might have been a Viking warrior in another life stepped forward to provide an escort. Even the steady Clarissa appeared entirely too pleased, which prompted Lady

Mallet to say, "I must go along. Laughlin, I expect you to watch over the others. Your sisters might fall off the parapet the way they are leaning against its edge."

"I suppose I must. Your hat, madam." He turned over the bonnet which had suffered a broken plume in its capture.

Regardless, she tied its ribbons tightly over her disarrayed coiffure and followed Clarissa and Grey like a bedraggled seabird. Lord Blackwater withheld his laughter only long enough for them to pass to the second story. "Damned amusing."

Entirely accustomed to their own father's oaths, the Longleigh twins faced into the wind and allowed it to rip the bonnets from their curly heads and hang by the strings. The state of their gowns bothered them not at all. "Wasn't that marvelous, James? We should encourage Papa to get some cannons," Clio said.

"Don't suggest it or we will have them on every hillock at Bellevue Hall with not an inch of seacoast to protect."

"I would gladly mount them on every wall of Castle Blackwater for you and your sister," Gareth proclaimed.

"And I'd help you set them off." Tristan offered.

"Enough! I mean, I think we've seen enough. Thank you for hospitality, Captain Thornton. We must be going." James moved forward to herd his sisters, but the Hardacre boys reached them first and helped them down to the next level. Thornton claimed the arm of Angelique, leaving him to follow with Lord Blackwater, that wretched man, smirking with glee.

~ * ~

Back at the castle, two enormous hampers stocked for the picnic awaited them on the trestle table. Out of one, a bottle looking suspiciously like a good French wine protruded. Lady Mallet pointed a long finger at its neck. "I find my nerves are entirely shattered by that cannon blast. I plan to dine in my chamber and lie down afterward to recuperate. Send along a bottle of that vintage if you have anymore. Laughlin, I put all of the girls in your charge." She left no time for him to answer before making for the stairs.

Why had he been deemed the chaperone of all four of them? Couldn't Blackwater—no, not a man to be trusted. Clarissa appeared to have some sense, but Angelique seemed to be swayed by every handsome face. His twin sisters were difficult to keep in order when they were up to mischief. Look at what he'd had to rescue Clio from at Almack's—Blandon's pawing and a near scandal.

Again, Lord Blackwater laughed in his sly way. "That woman has the right idea. I believe I'll go to bed with a bottle myself this afternoon and let you have the charge of all of them. An old man like me needs to rest for our next match this evening, Laughlin."

The Hardacre boys had already hefted the picnic baskets, but he signed for them to put them down. "Clio, Callie, go upstairs, change your gowns and put yourselves to rights. Ah, you also, Lady Angelique and Miss Downey." He knew he sounded exactly like a prissy governess or perhaps a mother trying to marry off four daughters at once.

With the temptation of the beach waiting, none of the girls were very long. They set off down the path James remembered as treacherous when he had ascended it after the grounding of his ship. On a spring day in broad daylight, it appeared much less threatening. The Hardacres led the way with a hamper on one arm and the twin of their choice on the other. Angelique clamped onto his arm as if someone had reminded her that the heir to a duke might be a better catch than a redcoat captain. She claimed a fear of heights, shrieked at every fallen pebble, and hugged closer. He'd offered Clarissa his free arm, but she'd proclaimed herself perfectly capable of walking down a path alone. He made certain she was wedged between him and the next Hardacre in case she slipped, but all arrived at the bottom unscathed. Sheltered by the rocky outcrops of the cliffs, the place proved pleasant enough on a clement day.

Since the girls had been stinted of their breakfast by Lady Mallet's departure, the blankets were quickly spread on the shingle and the hampers opened. Ham sandwiches of a size hardly dainty, a cold fowl, a jug of lemonade, the wine, cheeses and crackers, dried figs, and sweet biscuits made up their repast. Angelique asked her escort to cut the sandwiches and carve a leg off the fowl, which he did with a knife always carried in his boot. She found that as thrilling as the cannon blast and asked to hold the weapon in her hands before James cleaned it on a napkin and restored the knife to its place.

After eating, she suggested the ladies might like to wade in the surf. Sure she'd concocted a ploy to show off her fair ankles, James replied sourly that he knew the water to be too cold. Soon they would be calling him granny. Instead, they roamed the beach looking for perfect shells and any other curiosities the sea might yield. When Clio gave him the slip he was uncertain, but he noticed her absence and that of one of the Hardacres as they examined a decomposing creature the waves had washed in. Clarissa debated its origin with the remaining male twin. But where had Clio gone? He vowed never to have daughters!

~ * ~

Their escape had been so easy with Angelique clinging to James like an anchor and hampering him in every way. With a swift jerk of his head, Tristan caught Clio's eye, and she followed him through a narrow gap in a line of sea-smoothed boulders fallen from the cliff above. Surely, he meant to steal a kiss, but her chosen twin simply took her hand and led her behind yet another large rock. He bent low and entered a cave that gave Clio with her short stature no trouble at all. Above them, a small hole bored in the rock let in a stream of sunlight. It settled on crates and chests and small barrels all stacked neatly above the line where the water swirled at high tide.

"Aladdin's Cave," Clio breathed, "exactly like the one in *A Thousand and One Nights*."

"Hardly that," Tristan said. "You'll find no marvelous jinns in here to grant your every wish, only me and the other source of the Hardacre wealth. We leave the smugglers, Owlers we call them for the sounds they use to communicate, to their business, and they in turn leave part of their take here. We might be at war with France but the English still crave French luxuries, and the enemy is happy to have our wool in return. There is the source of the wine Lady Mallet identified so quickly." He pointed out a crate of bottles carefully nested in straw and turned on its side to allow extraction of its contents. Nearby, an open chest appeared to hold a new set of china very similar to the matching pieces used at breakfast and very possibly Limoges.

"When we were young lads, we discovered this place as we explored the shore. It proved a wonderful nook to hide from our father's frequent wrath, and look, has its own bolt hole." Tristan lifted down a heavy chest piled atop another that clanked with loose coinage and set it on floor of the cave revealing another hole that wormed its way into the cliff.

"Once past the opening, two boys could crawl on hands and knees to the other side and come out in a patch of bushes on the rear side of Marston. I suspect it started out a natural hole, but Owlers bored it through and set young boys on the other side to warn of any danger coming their way. We never touched their goods. It was our place in the daylight and theirs at night. Papa never knew where we'd turn up, this side of the cliff or the other, and it infuriated him. After he beat the truth out of us, he took up using it to hoard his own share of the goods."

"Our father would have thought us very clever and given us treats. Also, he has no objection to what he calls a little honest smuggling so long as it doesn't benefit Bonaparte."

"Time took care of our escape route, regardless. We'd be hard pressed to use it now with the size we've grown to."

"Yes," Clio said, tenderly placing a hand on his arm, but eyeing his broad shoulders. "I am so sorry for the way you were raised." She lifted her face to his, wanting to claim a kiss as good as the one Callie described, no, even better.

"Oh, there is worse, but I wanted to be honest with you in at least one way before…" He placed his hands on either side of her delicate collarbone and lowered his lips.

"Clio Longleigh, if you do not show yourself at once, we will all return to London immediately," James' voice boomed from somewhere above them.

They jumped apart as if he were right there within the cavern. "He must be standing on the boulders searching for us. We'll sneak out when he turns toward the sea. My father won't thank me for giving away the secret of the family's stash." Tristan stooped and peered through the opening. "Now, quickly!"

The couple squeezed round the boulder shielding the entrance and tumbled out onto the beach. They ran lightly down the shingle a few paces, turned, and pretended to be making their way back to the party of picnickers.

Clio gaily waved her hand at James who had indeed mounted the boulders to search for her. "We crossed over and walked a ways along the shore. Sorry to worry you, dearest brother."

James deftly leapt down practically in front of her. "If I had the time, I'd check your tracks."

"You couldn't on these stones," she answered with defiance.

"I could, but I've left the others alone. You make me shirk my duty."

"Here, the tide is still far enough out. Let me show you where we crossed." Tristan walked pointedly away from the cavern entrance and gestured to another break in the rocks, one that would be covered when the surf came up the shingle. It was a tight fit for the men, but not for Clio.

Their group emerged to find Angelique sulking on the picnic blanket and Clarissa reading from a pocket volume of poetry she'd brought along. Callie and Gareth walked near the edge of water where the white frills of the wavelets rushed to shore. They played a game where when it seemed as if Callie would wet her slippers, Gareth lifted her above the water and set her lightly down on dry land only to have Callie venture again too near the surf.

James narrowed his eyes at them and raised his voice in a tone that greatly resembled that of Miss Thurgood, their former governess. "Time to return to the castle!"

The others protested but he got his way as usual, his sisters said. As they trudged toward the pathway, he grumbled to Clarissa who seemed the only person with common sense. "Honestly, I've never seen men more eager to thrust their feet into marital leg shackles than these two. I hope they know what they are getting in Clio and Callie, a world of trouble."

"You see them with a brother's eyes, and they with a lover's longing glance."

He stared at the little volume of poetry she clutched. "Even you have been infected by Castle Blackwater." Reluctantly, he moved forward to offer his arm to the waiting Angelique who would snap the parson's mousetrap shut on his toes if she possibly could.

~ * ~

Rest and another change of clothes prepared everyone for dinner served by a bevy of Marston matrons in their Sunday best black dresses and spotless white aprons. Having gained some help in chopping and stirring from the scrawny daughters they'd brought along for the coin offered by Oskar, Bristol outdid himself to prepare a feast to rival any served in London. A clear soup to begin with and the chickens that provided the broth chopped fine into a pie for a later course, then the always superior fish a seaside town could provide. If the beef proved a little tough, the tiny lamb chops were tender. The women brought what greens they had in their gardens and happily sold to the castle kitchen. For pudding before the nuts and cheese, he'd put the young arms to work whipping the cream and making the custard for a trifle to be layered with strawberry jam and port-soaked sponge cake. Indeed, the length and breadth of the meal had all the guests groggy by the end of it.

Blackwater dominated the conversation as usual, this time boasting of his "allowing" the king's men to build a canal across his lands, another deterrent against a Napoleonic landing. James did not bother to repeat that no such invasion would occur. Lady Mallet encouraged the girls to speak enthusiastically about their afternoon on the beach if for no other apparent reason than to shut Lord Blackwater up for a few moments.

"Why, these delicate ladies must be exhausted from their day," Blackwater said with unusual concern for his company. "I suggest you retire early. We can enjoy your musical talents another night. Run along, children. Laughlin, might I engage you in another game of chess, played my way with a slight twist to make it far more interesting?"

"It would be my pleasure." James remained at the table as the others scurried off glad to be out of way of Lord Blackwater.

As the last of the skirts disappeared up the stairs, their host explained the new rules of chess. Whenever a man was taken from the board, the loser was required to quaff a cup of wine. James agreed to the terms. He'd played his share of drinking games as a student and traveler and mastered the art of appearing drunk long ago. If Blackwater wanted to win badly, so be it. He had no intention of dropping his guard in a place such as this castle. Playing poorly from the start, he polished off a cup or two, then allowed the dogs who had been let in after the ladies left to lap up his spillage from vessels knocked over or dribbled on the way to his lips. But he made shrewd moves often enough to dull Blackwater as well. Staggering hounds, a tipsy guest, and a lord as drunk as the proverbial one, brought the evening to a close when James paid up his wager and asked for Oskar's assistance in getting to his bed. He jolted against his sisters' doorway on his way up the stairs simply to let them know his whereabouts should they need him. Blackwater had been entirely too considerate tonight, another reason to beware.

Nineteen

Gareth Hardacre sat on the narrow step with his face sunk into his hands. Back braced against the wall of the staircase, Tristan occupied the space just beneath him. A small chunk of masonry kept the secret door behind the tapestry slightly ajar.

"Will they never stop reading this insipid tale?" Tristan grumbled in the lowest of whispers.

In the solar, the women had gathered together again to hear more of Walpole's tale of chivalry. Angelique read with great feeling.

"Hold gentle princess," said Theodore, "nor demean thyself before a poor and friendless young man. If heaven has selected me for thy deliverer, it will accomplish its work, and strengthen my arm in thy cause—".

Tristan snorted and stuffed his fingers in his ears. "Hush!" Gareth said.

"Did you hear something just now?" Callie asked.

"Only the wind soughing through this drafty chamber," Lady Mallet answered, tucking a coverlet higher under her armpits. "Go on, Angelique. You read so beautifully."

"I respect your virtuous delicacy," said Theodore; "nor do you harbour a suspicion that wounds my honour. I meant to conduct you

into the most private cavity of these rocks, and then, at the hazard of my life, to guard their entrance against every living thing. Besides, lady," continued he, drawing a deep sigh, "beauteous and all-perfect as your form is, and though my wishes are not guiltless of aspiring, know my soul is dedicated to another; and although"—a sudden noise prevented Theodore from proceeding.

"If we were only so lucky," Gareth murmured.

A pounding sounded on the chamber door. The ladies startled and squeaked in alarm.

"Have no fear, miladies. It's only Oskar come to light your way to bed. Lord Blackwater wants everyone up early for a ride before breakfast to sharpen your appetites. He promises Cookie will lay out a better spread tomorrow than today's porridge with honey."

Lady Mallet got to her feet and shoved them into her curly-toed slippers. She tightened the sash on her dressing gown. "Come along, Angelique and Clary. Who knows what great delicacy we will earn by going riding at an indecently early hour? Octopi served in their own ink, perhaps."

"Might we read only a little more, Mama?" Angelique begged.

"Oh," replied Clio. "Isabella swoons again at that noise just as she swooned when she beheld Theodore in the cavern. If I have any argument with this book, I'd say that entirely too much swooning goes on amongst the ladies. It is as if they have no spines to hold them up. However, a lengthy sword fight follows that, so we had better retire for the evening."

Reluctantly, Angelique turned over the volume to the twins. "How I'd like to have a man tell me my form is beauteous and all-perfect and that his soul is dedicated to me."

"Most certainly he'd be after your dowry as most men are who issue flowery compliments," Clarissa said. "I'd prefer a more plain-spoken man who simply said he loved me as I am."

"In your case, those compliments are sure to be scarce," Angelique retaliated.

"Girls, girls, girls, enough! Secure you wrappers before you step into the corridor. The castle ogre awaits us." Lady Mallet herded her charges before her, and their light footsteps pattered up the stairs.

"Callie, would you like to have a man's soul dedicated to you?" Clio asked as she snuffed the candle and settled in the bed.

"Oh my, yes!"

"Would you believe him?"

"If it were Tristan, I'd want to."

"His being a second son would not bother you in the least?"

"Not at all. He is gentle and true."

On the hidden staircase, Gareth nudged his brother's side with the toe of his boot. "As I said."

"Except you are not Tristan."

"Do you hear voices, Clio? Could the place be haunted by the ghost of the last marchioness or some other ancient lady?" Callie burrowed beneath the covers.

From the corridor, they both heard Oskar's deep voice. "Here we go, Lord Laughlin. But a few more steps and we'll be at your chamber. No need to feel embarrassed. Few can best Blackwater at drinking games. He wanted his chess wager back, you see."

Someone tripped outside their door, cursed and moved on. "Only James in his cups," Clio said as she snuggled next to her sister.

"That's odd. He rarely overindulges at home."

"He didn't show well when he went out with the Hardacre boys. I suspect he curbs himself because he doesn't hold his liquor all that exceptionally and wants no one to believe him less than perfect in anything. He won't be riding with us in the morning. We will be out from under his thumb for a change while he nurses a headache. Sweet dreams of knights and soul mates, Callie." The bed ropes twanged as she rolled over.

"Now?" asked Tristan.

"Soon. Let Oskar return and lock them all in their places."

Well-oiled earlier in the day, the lock clicked quietly as Oskar carried out the orders of Lord Blackwater. The girls did not stir. Gareth and Tristan pushed the secret door wider and stepped from behind the tapestry that rained a shower of dust on their shoulders. Tristan sneezed, and Clio sat bolt upright, her hand feeling beneath the pillow.

"Do not be alarmed! It is I, Gar, us, Tristan and Gareth," Gareth said quickly. He held up the lantern that had kept them company on the stairwell. "We want to escort you to someplace special through this secret passage behind the arras."

"Oh, then we must dress! Go out of the room again."

"I'd say come as you are," Tristan suggested with a wicked smile.

"Let them put on clothes against the chill, brother. We will go behind the tapestry, but wear something simple. Hurry!"

Gareth assumed his place behind the wall hanging and faced the stone blocks of the castle. Tristan applied his eye to a small moth hole in the weaving and observed as the young ladies shimmied from their night clothes and drew on chemises, stockings, and simple muslin dresses. From what he could tell, they were as identical naked as clothed, small yet—what had that fool Theodore said—beauteous and all-perfect from their rounded buttocks to their pert breasts. They bent over on the far side of the bed to secure their slippers, taking some time about it before turning his way again to tie their red and blue sashes for each other. Would they never be ready? Because he was, very ready.

"You can come out now," Clio called.

Callie walked unerringly to the twin she believed to be Tristan, whispering to her sister as she passed, "Our adventure begins."

Twenty

Down and down they went. One of the Hardacres led the way with a lantern. The other brought up the rear with another light as the girls made their way carefully on the crumbling steps. They passed a small landing and another secret door, but kept moving. The air grew warm as they descended to the kitchen level, then colder again as the stairs burrowed deeper into the rock. At last, they came to an abrupt end in a circular space that seemed to have no exit. Gareth Hardacre removed a brick-sized stone, and a door disguised by a thin a layer of masonry swung open with no difficulty as if it had been used often and serviced recently. He and his brother bade the ladies enter first.

"A subterranean chamber," Callie breathed.

"A dungeon," Clio said with some grumpiness. "This is what you wanted to show us in the middle of the night? Couldn't we have come down here in the morning?"

"You sound like Lady Mallet or James. Oh, but a nighttime visit makes it all the more delicious. Do show us around." Callie clapped her hands in delight.

Gareth and Tristan held their lanterns high to reveal all a true dungeon should possess: rusting manacles hanging from the walls like skeletal bones, an iron boot to crush the feet of those reluctant to divulge a secret, a rack that had become a home to spiders and their webs, and a brazier still holding bits of charcoal and a branding iron in its bowl as if the head torturer had simply stepped out for his dinner and would return shortly. All of them jumped when Oskar stepped from the first of a row of cells. With his leather eye patch and brawny arms, he fit easily into the role of the missing tormenter. Holding the heavy door open, he beckoned to the first couple.

"Enter your chamber for the night. The straw is fresh as is the water. I've bunged up any rat holes. You will be undisturbed and safe for the evening, I promise you. My boys will do right by their ladies." His speech became an anxious innkeeper more than a dungeon master rather ruining the fun.

Clio walked boldly into the cell and twirled around. "This is the secret—we are to spend the night here with you guarding over us like true knights over beautiful captives."

Tristan followed her and hung the lantern on a hook as he entered. "Not exactly." Knowing no better way to start, he began with the kiss James had aborted in the beach cave. Clio stepped into his embrace. Both were only distantly aware of the others moving off to another cell. His lips moved over hers, not gently but with urgency and passion. The stiffening of her nipples against his chest and the heat gathering between her legs where his manhood pressed encouraged him even more. He stripped the red ribbon from the end of her hair neatly plaited by Finch before bedtime and tossed it in the straw. His fingers raked through her curls, parting, snarling, sometimes hurting her in his hurry.

Clio gave him a reminder to be gentler. She worked her fingers beneath his jacket and waistcoat and under the long tails of his shirt. Making her way upward, she scored his right shoulder with her nails and dug into the left. Rather than stop him, her little act of vengeance inflamed his desire. "Yes," he said. "Yes. Mark me as your own."

But her left hand dropped, and her mouth broke away from his. "You already bear a mark, a deep one. What is it?"

Emitting a sigh that came out more like a moan, he stepped back. "I meant to tell you first but got carried away. At the age of twelve, my father set that very branding iron against my flesh as Oskar held me down at his command. He said he would no longer be fooled as to which of us was his true heir. We'd switched roles on him one too many times." As he talked, Tristan tore away his neckcloth, shed his jacket and waistcoat, and pulled his shirt down over one shoulder. He turned his back on Clio and revealed the brand II.

"Two? The Roman number two? But you are the first born."

Restoring his shirt, he faced her. "No, I am Tristan, the second son. That can never be changed. Gareth allowed me to assume his title in London so that I might enjoy the adulation. It is not to his taste, you see. I reveled in it, the fawning over the heir of a marquess, the pursuit of the young women who wanted me for a husband."

"Stupidly, I was one of those. How could I allow this to happen?" Clio made for the thick door of the cell and found it locked. She rattled the small bars set into an opening to permit the jailer to see inside the cell and stained her hands with rust. "Oskar, I want to leave now! Open this door immediately."

She turned at a rustling in the straw and thought immediately of rats but found Tristan huddled in the thick bedding with his arms about his bent knees and his head lowered. "He will not return until morning upon my father's orders. We are expected to—to force ourselves on our would-be brides in order to bring off an immediate marriage. As he reminded me, no young lady with your options will choose a penniless second son otherwise."

"How could I? How could I?" Clio repeated, wringing her hands and wiping them on her white skirts as if she tried to removed blood rather than rust. "You were the one who led the way, the more aggressive like any heir to a great fortune. How could I?"

Tristan's head snapped up. Her words scored more deeply than her nails. The depth of his hurt burned more than his branding. "Indeed, how could you pursue a title and wealth just like any of the other girls brought out this year? Your brother told me that was all the Season amounted to, and I see now it is true. Honest affection and admiration are overridden by money and status. I thought you might be different."

"You—you plan to rape me, and you speak of honest affection. You flirted with more women than me." Clio pointed a quivering finger at him and stayed with her back pressed to the door as if rescue might come at any minute.

"To make you jealous and more eager to have me. I hoped you would come to me willingly, though I understand many women cry rape afterwards." He let his disgust show in his tone.

"How could I?" Clio asked once more.

"Because you are like all the others, like Lady Angelique clinging to Laughlin or Blandon or the one she thought might be Viscount Marston, so desperate to attain the best title."

"Would you stop assuming you know me so well? A Longleigh woman is like no other. What I cannot believe is how could I have fallen in love with a second son so strongly I am actually considering going through with this fantasy."

Clio moved forward and lowered herself next to him in the straw. Below the prickly chaff, lay a soft pallet obviously provided by Oskar for their comfort. She worked the shirt off his shoulders, above his head, and tossed it aside. "Let me see the scar more closely."

"You are as bold as I believed you to be. I'm not wrong about that at least." He allowed the examination.

Clio ran her fingers over the mark, and he shook beneath her hand. "Are you cold, Gar—Tristan?"

"Cold and hot all at the same time."

Her hands moved over his chest, covering his puckered nipples. She pressed herself against him as if sharing her body heat. His lips descended again and when the kiss at length ended, her naked breasts warmed his hands.

"Are you ready and willing to go farther, my love?" he asked.

"I believe I understand for the first time that desire burns in the strangest of places. Go on."

He laid her back gently in their odd private bower and ran his hands beneath her skirts. "What's this I find instead of smooth, rosy flesh?"

"Oh, the stiletto I would have killed you with had you forced yourself upon me. Papa has supplied all his daughters with them."

"Would you mind if I laid it aside?"

"I'd rather you let it be—in case I change my mind."

"It certainly adds spice to seduction that I might die at any moment."

Impatient, Clio wiggled her hips in the straw. "Could we get on with it? I've read some rather naughty books that call the sexual act the little death and wish to know if that is true."

"Extraordinary. Let me ready you first to ease the way."

"I am ready now!"

"Says the innocent virgin. No need to rush. We have all night."

His hands moved beyond cold steel to her hot core where the dampness between her thighs nearly convinced him to enter her at once, but no. He should take time with her as he would with a spirited but nervous filly he wanted to train to the saddle. He tested with one finger first, then two, stretching her a little, preparing her. With her own slickness, he tormented the small nub at her apex with his thumb.

Clio no longer talked or insisted. She simply writhed and arced. His pleasure came in watching her when she experienced the ultimate delight for the first time. Her dark eyes closed, her mouth panted, her tinted skin took on deeper color as she gasped and uttered the small sounds of the sexually entranced. When he ceased tormenting her to the pinnacle of joy, Clio sunk back limply against the pallet, much of the straw having been pushed aside by her actions.

"That was sublime. Are we finished? Women seem to make so much of losing their maidenheads that I expected pain, not pleasure."

"Unfortunately, we are not done, but I will make it fast. I could hardly do otherwise considering I might burst my buttons any minute."

"Burst your buttons?" Tristan moved one of her small hands to the hardness of his crotch to show his urgency. "Oh, I see. You haven't had your turn yet."

"Very perceptive. Those who taught me would be impressed I've held back this long, but in Castle Blackwater, you gain skill in three things: fighting, drinking, and well, this. Release me, Clio." He guided her hands to open his flap. Her fingers strayed to touch the length of him from tip to root as he sprang free.

"A Longleigh woman is never afraid," she murmured.

"She does not need to be. It will fit. Enough conversation. I cannot hold back anymore if you keep touching me." He clutched her hands and moved them to his shoulders, then bending, took her in one swift deep move. She did not scream, just tightened around him and brought him to a sudden release, but he did cry out, short and sharp. Tristan bowed over her, took her lips, and remained mated to her hips until she relaxed again. Slowly, he withdrew.

"Next time will be better, I promise." He lay down beside her and cradled her languidly against his steaming chest. "As soon as my legs will hold me, I will wash you. Oskar, that romantical fool, has left us water, toweling, and if my senses don't deceive me, scented soap."

"Sounds lovely, being washed by you, my dearest. I think I begin to understand why my parents spend so much time in their bed napping."

That made him laugh. "I doubt they nap at all." Tristan forced himself to tuck in and arise from their warn nest to soak a cloth and lave it between her legs. His attentions stirred her. She moaned and sighed loudly as he applied the slippery fabric smelling of roses more firmly until she arched again.

"Marvelous," Clio said. "I suppose I am my mother's daughter."

Tristan returned the cloth to the basin. "Clio, I thank you for accepting a second son."

He said it with such humility she smiled, then sat up abruptly. "Callie, I haven't thought of her once this whole time!"

"I don't think most women dwell on their sisters while they are being deflowered."

"But we do everything together! I haven't heard a sound from the other cell. Do you think Gareth has raped her?"

"Gareth, no! He truly is the perfect knight. If he can bring himself to do it at all, he would do so gently. By now your sister might be a future marchioness."

"And precede me at all occasions."

"I'm afraid so."

"I find I don't care in the least. Come lie with me again, Tristan Hardacre. We have all night." Clio patted the pallet, and he came to her swiftly.

Twenty-one

Callie tilted her head at Gareth. "Are we truly locked in here for the night? No help will come if I scream and shout?"

"No help will come. My father is very unkind to those who oppose his plans. But keep your voice very low. Do not give him the satisfaction of believing you are terrified if he listens somewhere nearby. Our dear Papa thrives on the fear of others."

"I am not terrified. I trust you in every way. Won't James be furious when he finds out we've spent the evening together here and must marry?" Her excitement triggered his.

"You don't object then to being forced to take a second son as a husband?"

"Clio might, but not me. I've thought from the first you were not the heir and yet you pleased me more and more with your gentility. If I can live here with you, Clio and Gareth, all my days, I would be content."

"And with my father?"

"Perhaps we should keep a place in the city, too. My dowry will permit it."

His blue eyes lit as if a sunbeam slanted across the waters. "That will not be necessary as I am the true heir, Calliope Longleigh. My brother and I switched places in London. He wanted to experience what being the firstborn was like. I wanted to find a love true to the man, not his wealth or title. You passed the test."

In the lantern light, her eyes blazed like two small fires lit against the darkness. "You were testing us! Suppose I don't care for the results. I have no desire to be a marchioness and lord it over one and all. Clio will be crushed when she learns of this as she wanted the position so badly."

"More to your credit that you think of your sister at a time like this. If your sister does not accept Tristan as he is, my brother will live the rest of his life in bitterness. His love for her is deeper than he will admit."

Callie kicked at the bed of straw and sent the chaff flying. "You should have thought of that before concocting this ridiculous adventure."

"I did not concoct it. My father demanded we do this to secure our brides. It was to go further than simply a night spent together. He plotted your rape. And I have to say this situation is no more ridiculous than the one in the book you are reading. If you believe so strongly in dedicated souls and true love, you have found it in me." Exasperated, he held out his arms inviting her to come to him.

Callie stayed where she stood. "I have to admit *The Castle of Otranto* does not end happily. Theodore loves Matilda, but when she is stabbed to death by her own father, he marries Isabella so he can spend the rest of his life remembering her with his wife who loved her also. I wouldn't want an ending like that. I don't desire Tristan's eternal bitterness because of the trick you have played or to spend my life speaking to my sister of the man I might have had if I hadn't turned from him at this minute." She moved into his arms. "If I am willing, then it is not rape."

"Your brother might not see it that way, but then he could kill me simply for lying beside you. If I had a sword, I would put it between us on the pallet to show my true intention to marry you without stealing what is most precious to a woman until offered on the wedding night."

Callie pulled away and turned her back on him. She turned swiftly with a stiletto drawn and pointed at Gareth. He backed away, hands in the air. Smiling at her own trick, she said, "Would a dagger do? My father insisted his daughters never go out into society unprepared to defend themselves." She turned the blade and handed it to him hilt first. He accepted her offer but laid the knife aside on a narrow ledge.

"You continue to surprise me. May it remain that way all of our lives. But I can offer another alternative." Gareth swept aside the straw and pushed the pallet aside. He delved into a corner and removed a stone.

From a hidden niche, he withdrew an impressive key and offered it to her. "Freedom of choice. Our father often locked us in this cell as a punishment for any infraction he might imagine. It is the last in the row, the darkest and most distant from the entry. We were expected to cower here all night in misery, but Oskar, bless his soft heart, could not bear it. He had a duplicate key made and hidden here. We were free to escape and go where we liked for the night, usually to Mother Grubbs, provided we were back before dawn to pathetically beg release from our father."

"Mother Grubbs? Was she a kindly lady who provided you with a warm bed?" Callie asked, all her sympathies engaged.

"One might say. Let's speak of other things. Do I lie beside you, never touching you all through the night, or do we take the key, release ourselves and return you and your sister to your bedchamber unmolested with none the wiser?" He awaited her answer with patience as she did not speak at once.

Callie, the thoughtful one, pondered. "If we return to our beds and are found there in the morning, your father will be wroth with you."

"Foaming at the mouth angry, I imagine, at letting our chance to secure a wealthy heiress slip away. I don't know what he might do, he is that unpredictable. When Tristan and I switched roles early in our youth to confound him, he dragged us both here and heated a branding iron made to order some time before. He wanted to know which of us was truly his heir. Neither of us spoke up, so he grabbed me and bared my back to have the Roman number II burned into my flesh. Then Tristan answered, admitting he was the second son, and took my place. He bears the mark to this day."

Callie shuddered in a way that had nothing to do with the chill in the dungeon. "Your father is mad, cruel and mad." She moved close, and he enfolded her in his arms.

"I will risk his wrath for you."

"No, I want lie beside you this night and all others. Will we truly wed in the morning?"

"He means to release us at dawn and have the vicar waiting. Lady Mallet and the other girls are locked in their chamber, but I suspect he might trot them down here to witness your fall from grace. Laughlin is far too dangerous. My father made sure your brother overindulged in drink before going to bed and has also locked him in the alchemist's chamber, no other exit from there but the top of the tower. We ride to the church in the early morn and marry, returning to deliver the news as a fait accompli. I swear it on the crossed hilt of this stiletto." He wrapped a hand around the knife as he made his oath and then drove it into the pallet.

"My perfect knight," said Callie as he knelt to build up the bedding for her and helped her to lie down to one side of the knife. Gareth took the place nearest the wall and added the key to the barrier between them. Both lay on their backs with their hands crossed over their bosoms. Neither slept.

Callie's hand moved to wrap around the key. His thigh pressed hard against the cold metal of the stiletto reminding him to keep his place. The dungeon filled with echoing sighs and moans and one sharp cry. She released the key and found his hand.

"I do believe the ghosts of those who were tormented here walk tonight."

Gareth answered that remark with a low chuckle. "Mortals in ecstasy made those sounds, not the dead. I believe Clio and my brother have reached an understanding."

"You mean they have experienced the little death together?"

"What? Not death, but the essence of life."

"Just a term for physical release. The library at Bellevue Hall is remarkably complete if one takes the time to look on all the top shelves. When I come to think about it, I've heard those noises often enough coming from my parents' bedchamber, only louder. It all makes sense I see, those long naps they take. But now Clio knows something I don't. I find I am jealous and intrigued."

Gareth did not miss his chance. "Enough to experience the same?"

"Yes, once we get all this metal off the bed."

She tossed the key aside, and he threw the knife into a corner. They came together with the passion of two people who had been contemplating consummation for some time. In fact, Gareth found Callie on top sitting astride the seat of his desire as she tore at his clothes trying to undo the knot of his neckcloth that Oskar had tied that morning. Failing in that, she began on the buttons of his jacket and waistcoat with more success.

Gareth stayed her hands. "Steady, dear Calliope. The dungeon is cold and damp, and we need not be entirely unclothed for this. In fact, it would better if I took the upmost position this time. No need for you to learn to ride astride right now."

"Papa always says Englishmen wear too many clothes. I believe that is true. He let us ride our ponies astride and barebacked when we were young, but Mama put a stop to it fearing we'd become bowlegged and have female problems. Papa claims the Shawnee women did so and are not bowlegged." In an attack of nerves, she continued to babble.

Gareth shifted her small body to the side and laid her back in the straw. "Perhaps less talk about your father at this moment. The thought shrivels me."

"Well, he did once kill and scalp a man he thought took my mother's honor, but it had nothing to do with riding astride."

"It might if you rode astride me and not a pony, Callie."

"Oh, I see." In the dim lantern light, her cheeks darkened.

"For tonight we will not disrobe, but tomorrow in our warm bed as man and wife I will glory in your nakedness. Quiet for now. Let me prepare you. I want to dedicate my body and soul to you." Take that Horace Walpole. He must have found the right words because she sighed deeply and parted her limbs for him.

Mumbling about the number of clothes women wore even when lightly clad, he found his way through the maze of her skirts and undergarments to rest his hand on her mound, hot and covered in soft curls, but not yet ready to receive him. He slid his finger in her cleft and massaged the button of flesh at its top. Her eyes closed and her mouth parted, but no words escaped. She grew slick beneath his touch. He unbuttoned and replaced his fingers with his hardened shaft, stroking gently back and forth until she moaned and tossed.

Ever so slowly, he entered her, waited for her acceptance, then went another inch. Startled when she grabbed his buttocks, he plunged forward faster than intended. She did gasp before relaxing beneath him. In to the hilt, he continued his conquest until Callie bowed against him and found her release. He surged on until he joined her in ecstasy. The little death, indeed. More like a cataclysm. He rested his head over her quick-beating heart for a moment.

"Are you well?" he asked in concern.

"More than well. Astounded. Pleasured, I think is the term."

"My pleasure also. After we rest, I think we should release Clio and Tristan and thwart my father's plans by beating him to the vicar. I will not have the two of you embarrassed and humiliated. We will wed and return to the castle as couples who could not restrain their passion and eloped."

"That, my love, would be true enough." Callie stroked his side whiskers with her fingertips as she might a favorite cat and soon slept nestled on his chest.

He did not allow her to rest long. His father might change plans on a whim or be waiting nearby. Carefully, he shifted his beloved's curly head to the pallet and went to find the key thrown aside so carelessly not too long ago. He came across the knife first and nicked his finger in the process, but it mattered little. The key lay just beyond it. He opened the heavy cell door before waking his Calliope and helping her put herself to rights, all straw removed from her locks and backside.

He'd buttoned his pants, but she restored his waistcoat and jacket. Considering each other, they proclaimed themselves ready to escape.

"Unless you wish to wash with the rosewater Oskar left."

"Oh, I would. I never knew the sexual act had an odor."

"A very distinct one. Take your time."

Turning her back, she modestly raised the front of her skirts and cleansed herself. She also resheathed her stiletto. "As Papa says, one never knows when it might come in handy." Ready, she gave Gareth her hand and prepared to disturb her sister.

At the door to the other cell, Gareth peered inside and blocked Callie's view. "They are in more dishabille than us. Give them a moment to right themselves. Psst! Tristan, awake. Have you forgotten the key? We are going to make our escape."

A gruff voice from the cell answered. "Go away. The deed is done. She accepts me as her mate. Let us enjoy the rest of this night together."

"Dress, I say!" Gareth had caught sight of a delight he'd denied himself, Clio's naked brown breasts and shapely bared legs, presumably identical to Callie's attributes. His brother, bare-chested and buttoned askew, held his twin in his arms. For a moment, he forgot about noble acts and wished he'd left the key buried. No help for it now. "Come, would you allow our father to humiliate the women we love in the morning? I say we go right now and rouse the preacher to marry us, then return to the castle in our own good time. We are at his mercy no longer. These women have set us free of him! We need not live at Castle Blackwater ever again."

"If you say so, milord. Allow the peasants a moment to comply with your orders, sire. Clio, Clio, we must prepare to go, my brother says. Away to the chapel right now to marry."

The straw rustled. "Can't it wait until morning?"

"No, Clio, it cannot," Callie said, trying to peep past Gareth's broad shoulders by standing on her tiptoes. He continued to block her way. "We need to make this seem an elopement completed before James is released. He prides himself on being more civilized than Papa, but I suspect he is not."

"True enough. Give us a moment."

The other couple finally appeared, still considerably more mussed than their counterparts. Callie plucked straw from Clio's hair and Gareth pointed out his brother's ill-buttoned flap. Finally satisfied, they returned to the secret staircase and followed it upwards to another bolt hole that opened beside the great hearth in the kitchen. Sneaking past the snoring Oskar draped over the sill to the room where Finch slept and the two turnspit dogs who barely raised their heads after an exhausting day of running on the wheel, they lifted the bar across the rear entrance and escaped into the night, two sets of lovers bent on marriage.

Twenty-two

Clarissa Downey could not sleep. The castle walls seemed filled with noises: the whispers of past doomed lovers, the ghostly light footsteps of deceased children, the heavy tread of men in boots long dead. If a giant helmet fell from the sky into the courtyard on the viscount's wedding day as it had in *The Castle of Otronto,* she would not have been surprised. What nonsense! When an entirely modern case clock chimed one somewhere deep in the fortress, she determined to rise and quietly read some less fabulous tale from the selection she'd brought along to entertain herself.

Taking care not to awaken Lady Mallet and Angelique who slept in her mother's arms, Clarissa slipped carefully from her side of the marquess's large bed and made her way to the chair by the brazier. She stirred its coals and lit a candle with an ember. Bother, where were her glasses? Ah, she'd left them in the twins' chamber again. Drawing on a pair of slippers and planning to be in and out of the room below without waking the other girls, she made for the heavy door. Someone had been round with an oil can because it had ceased to creak when they entered tonight rather than the screech it had made the previous evening. She expected it to open softly, but it did not open at all. A brisk rattling of the latch helped not one bit, but it did rouse Lady Mallet.

"Whatever are you doing, Clarissa? Come back to bed this minute, or I shall never get my full rest," the woman said, as if she hadn't napped with that bottle of wine all afternoon.

"I wanted to retrieve my spectacles without disturbing anyone, but we appear to be locked in this evening."

"Nonsense. No one bothers to lock doors at a country seat. It is simply too inconvenient with all the comings and goings of servants and lov...others. The thing is merely stuck." Flouncing from the bed, she gave the recalcitrant door a good shove and ended rubbing her shoulder. "Perhaps you are right."

"I wonder if the twins are also locked away."

"If we can't go to them, we shan't know."

"Oh, the floor timbers have shrunken over the years and the marquess is using rugs to cover the cracks. I tripped over one just yesterday and exposed a gap. Help me roll this one up."

Lady Mallet agreed, but stopped short of lying on the floor to peer through the exposed opening. Clarissa did the honors. "Callie, Clio, are you awake? Are you locked in?"

No answer. She spoke louder and only managed to end Angelique's slumber. "Who cares at this hour? Someone will be by in the morning to open the lock."

"Because I have a hunch—or a portent of doom as Walpole might say. Something is going to happen this evening." Clarissa scanned more of the room below. Two white garments lay cast carelessly aside on the floor. "I see two nightdresses flung about."

"Their maid will see to it later," Angelique answered sleepily.

"So you believe the Longleigh girls sleep in the nude, do you?"

"Little about them would surprise me, but no. Drafty as this place is, we should have brought flannel rather than cotton," Lady Mallet said with a shiver.

"They have gone out—or were taken away. We must alert their brother at once," Clarissa insisted.

"If we are locked in, how shall we do that?" Angelique burrowed farther into the covers.

"Oh, for pity's sake! We still have our voices and a poker left by the brazier." Clarissa got to her feet, retrieved the poker, and began banging it on a ceiling made of ancient wood not any different from their flooring. Little bits of it splintered off under her vigorous assault making a hole a little wider. "Wake up, Lord Laughlin. We are locked in, and your sisters have disappeared from their chamber."

Heavy boots hit the floor above. A latch rattled. A blow to a door sounded. A curse followed. Clarissa applied the poker again. "Here, you can converse with us through this hole." She thrust the poker into the gap raising a carpet above.

James pushed the tip of it down with his boot and a moment later, his gray eye appeared in the crack. "The good Lord Jesus, Miss Downey, you nearly impaled my foot with that thing. Put it down! I, too, am incarcerated, but I have an interior stair to the top of the tower. I shall lower myself to your window. From there, we will proceed. Prepare for my entry."

"Oh," squeaked Angelique. "You will dash yourself to death on the stones of the courtyard."

"Not if I am careful. Open the window and stand aside."

Before Clarissa could obey his orders, Lady Mallet insisted they all don their dressing gowns and cover their feet for the sake of decency. A search ensued for slippers lost under the bed and wrappers left in odd places. Their efforts ended when a great thud sounded against the barred window and a stream of invective sure to warm at least their ears followed. "Open the window!"

Clarissa hurried to remove the bar and fling open the wooden shutters. On the other side, James Longleigh hung from a knotted rope of bed linens. "Finally! I'm going to swing myself inside."

He pushed off against the sill and on the return arc inserted his legs through the opening. All went well until his broad shoulders stuck. "Draw me inside, for God's sake!"

"Take his limbs and pull," Clarissa said as she began to tug on one leg. His boot came off in her hands. She yanked at his muscular calf instead. Somewhat reluctant, Angelique gave a timid little jerk on the other leg.

"Stand aside. This is a job for a grown woman." Lady Mallet applied her bulk to the situation and with some hunching and scraping, James Longleigh entered their domain like an infant after a hard birth. "There now, daughter, isn't this far more dashing than a man in a scarlet uniform?"

"I suppose," Angelique answered her mother with some doubt as James replaced his boot and frowned at his jacket with the elbows torn out. His wine-stained shirt and waistcoat hardly added a jot to his heroic image, though he had managed to transport a slim sword with him by holding it along one leg.

He dusted his hands. "Now to find a way out of here." He began searching behind the tapestries and found nothing. "In these novels you read, isn't there always a hidden staircase?"

"Or a trapdoor or a subterranean chamber," Angelique supplied helpfully.

"A trapdoor! I've noticed a different sound when I walk past the foot of the bed. Seek under that carpet," Clarissa suggested.

They bared a trapdoor with an iron ring inset to raise it. "Excellent," James exclaimed. "Good work, Miss Downey." For all of her good sense, she could not suppress a blush at his compliment.

"Now, I'm going to jump down. It isn't far. Perhaps I can discover what became of my sisters." Bunching his knees, he propelled himself from the edge of the opening and tore through the canopy of one of the beds. The ropes holding up the mattress held, and he bounced, laughing, deep into the feather tick. "Very easy. Anyone else coming?"

"Me!" How could she resist? Without hesitation Clarissa launched her thin and usually clumsy body straight as an arrow through the hole. James caught her in his arms and set her aside. Her cheeks flamed anew.

"Anyone else?"

"Go along, Angelique. Fly into Laughlin's arms," Lady Mallet prompted. "I shall go last."

"I'm not sure that I want..." A firm push from her mother sent her on her way. She landed without mishap still standing and needed only his steadying of her elbow before she climbed from the bed.

"Here I come, Laughlin!" Lady Mallet threw herself into the gap with abandon. James caught her, issuing an "oomph" as he did. The bed ropes at last gave way and the frame collapsed beneath them, leaving the couple entangled in a welter of sheets and blankets. They crawled from the wreckage. Flushed, Lady Mallet rose and fanned her broad bosom with a hand. "Thrilling, so very thrilling."

Clearly unhappy, James Longleigh went first to the door and found it locked. He eyed his sister's nightdresses crumpled in a heap. Stalking across the room, he began another inspection of the wall hangings. Clarissa walked heavily on the floorboards trying to discern another trapdoor. Angelique and her mother mainly watched. On his third try, James turned back the unicorn beguiled by the maiden and found the secret door. He drew his boot knife, useful for more than slicing sandwiches, and probed into the crack until he found a latch to raise on its blade.

"I believe we've found how my sisters left this chamber, whether voluntarily or kidnapped. I'm following this staircase to its bottom." He lit a candle at their brazier and started off, leaving the women to decide on their own if they would follow. Determined not to be left behind on this glorious adventure, Clarissa ignited a second candle and entered the downward passage.

"Hurry, Angelique, or they will get too far ahead." Lady Mallet cried as she set flame to another taper and stood in the secret doorway.

"I believe I shall stay here, Mama. It's all well and good when adventures are between the covers of a book, but I think I do not care for them for real."

"And let Laughlin alone with Clarissa? Never." She thrust her candle at her daughter and selected another for herself. They descended the steep staircase with four candles lighting their way. Laughlin stopped at each landing and raised the latches. In the great hall, Blackwater, too drunk to acknowledge a few warning woofs, snored in a pile of his dogs. The next revealed the kitchen smelling pleasantly of sugar and spice and a bowl of raisins soaking in brandy. At the far end, Oskar slept restless on his pallet with the turnspit dogs for company. The last exit stood wide open to a dungeon, chill and dark, yet possessing an unexpected odor of ripeness and roses.

Sniffing the air as keen as one of the castle hounds, James moved immediately toward one of the open cells. He kicked aside the straw and studied a small stain on the pallet beneath it. With one furious swipe of his hand, he overturned a basin of rose-scented water and kicked it against the wall. Clarissa, who had ranged out on her own, called from the far cell, "I've found some blood droplets, still fairly fresh."

He went to the second scene at once. Peering close over his shoulder, Lady Mallet said holding up her candle, "Ordinary blood from a cut, Laughlin, not the sort that indicates a torn maidenhead. Look for that on the pallet."

He did and found his evidence. Stepping from the cell, he headed for the secret staircase. Lady Mallet's sharp voice stopped him. Her eyes, cold and blue, gleamed above her candle with the satisfaction of a wolf about to down its prey.

"Either your sisters were ravished or gave themselves willingly to the Hardacre boys without benefit of marriage. I have seen the evidence with my own eyes. I would suspect the vile old man, but he sleeps above too drunk to perform. Your mother will never overcome this scandal."

James met her eyes, his own like the hard, gray stones of the castle walls. "Who is to know if none of us tells the tale?"

"Word gets around. Now, if you were my future son-in-law, I would forever be obliged to keep this secret in the family. Otherwise I must warn society of loose women in their midst."

James froze like an animal about to meet its doom but too paralyzed to run. A high voice behind him said, "Yes, we must warn society of loose women. I saw with my very own eyes Lady Mallet tussling in the bedclothes with Lord Laughlin at Castle Blackwater. People might believe she wants him as a son-in-law only to carry on an affair." Clarissa had seen all, heard all, and made her statement.

James turned and offered her a smile worthy of heartbreak, but she steeled herself. The likes of James Longleigh were not for her and did not fit into her future plans already made.

"You ungrateful child! I offered to chaperone your visit here. Of course, you had no hope of the Hardacre twins, but I thought perhaps the father would not be too picky, disgusting as he is. This is how you repay my care—with a terrible fabrication." Lady Mallet bristled, a cat whose mouse had just escaped its claws.

"My statement is true at least, no matter how it is interpreted. We do not know what became of Clio and Callie, and I suggest we withhold judgment until we do," Clarissa replied evenly.

"I intend to do exactly that. Ladies, you can find your way back to the bedchamber, I trust. Oskar will know what happened here. I have no more time to waste. Miss Downey, if ever you are in need of a favor—short of marriage—I am at your service." James Longleigh bowed, turned on his heels, and disappeared into the bolt hole.

Clarissa's hand strayed to her heart. Here ended the most exciting chapter of her life.

~ * ~

The kitchen dogs ran to cower under a table when the booted feet headed their way. Oskar awoke with the pressure of a knife tip against his remaining good eye. It rolled wildly in its socket, but his large body remained absolutely still. His thick lips hardly moved as he murmured, "What is it you want, milord?" to the looming James Longleigh.

"The whereabouts of my sisters and your young masters. I've been to the dungeon and seen the evidence of their debauchery. Someone will die tonight for this, but it need not be you if you make your confession right now."

"Not my plan, nor the boys. The marquess demanded they claim their brides tonight in the way he took his, but I know Gareth and Tristan. They would not rape but rather persuade because they do love and honor your sisters. A marriage ceremony is planned in the morning. I swear me sight on it. Where they are now, I do not know. They were to remain locked in the cells until morning."

A small but strong hand grabbed James' wrist and yanked it upward. "Do not threaten him! He serves an evil master the same as these turnspit dogs work for the cook without choice. If the deed is done, the church will remedy the situation. Know your sisters have great affection for these young men whom I trust will be honorable." Finch, shivering in her night shift so hard even the thick brown braid slung over her shoulder quivered, did not remove her staying hand, though James could have wrenched it free whenever he wished.

"I must find them and make certain of their safety. They are my responsibility, Finch."

"I left soft pallets and scented water for them and a means to escape if the old key remained in its hiding place, but they were to stay the night and be discovered by his lordship come dawn. Then to the vicar for a hasty wedding and back here for a wedding breakfast. Can't ye smell Bristol's preparations? I swear this is the truth." Oskar pressed is hands together in supplication now that the knife had been removed.

"Perhaps they used that key and made their own decision to wake the vicar," Finch suggested.

"Where might I find this vicar?"

"At the far end of Marston in the stone house of two stories next to the chapel. Can't miss it, but I'll gladly show ye the way," Oskar volunteered as he moved to his knees. He sloughed off his blankets and emerged fully dressed except for a neckcloth. "Go back to bed, Miss Finch. I'll see our youngsters safe."

"You had better, or I'll be the one threatening you with a knife," she answered. "As if I can sleep now!"

Oskar hung his head, but James beckoned him to the unbarred kitchen door. "Someone has already passed this way tonight."

"Our twins, for certain our twins."

The two men in search of a pair of runaway lovers made for the stables to pursue them.

Twenty-three

Without rousing the stable boy who slept on a cot amidst the tack, Gareth and Tristan had saddled their own horses and lifted the girls to ride a pillion behind them down the castle pathway. Each had wrapped their lady in their jackets against the damp of the evening and their bodies pressed close for more warmth or perhaps simply out of desire. A full moon lit their path through the rusty portcullis and along the steep and crooked lane to Marston. They passed the bawdyhouse with light still escaping around its shutters and laughter seeping into the night air.

Tristan jested that it spoke to the character of past lords that a house of ill-repute sat closer to the castle than the church, but none of them laughed. The rest of the village showed no sign of life at this hour. The ordinary folk saved their rush lights and cheap tallow candles by going to bed early and staying there until dawn. A few dogs barked but recognized the men and horses that passed by and soon settled.

At the vicarage, Gareth pounded on the green door until an upper window raised and the balding priest stuck out his head out dangerously into the miasmas of the night. He wore a nightcap tied beneath his doubled chin, and a prosperous belly strained his shirt.

"Does someone at the castle require last rites immediately, or can he wait until a more decent hour? Men of God need their rest, too, you know."

"We wake you for a far more joyous reason," Gareth said. "We wish to wed these ladies immediately."

"Ah, *those* ladies. His lordship said I was to perform the double ceremony after the eight of the clock Mass. I suppose he intends to pay for the special licenses I've sent for after the fact. Not good to cheat the church. I am already bending the rules and have no wish to twist them further at this outrageous hour. Return at eight." The sash slammed down and did not rise again no matter how hard they pounded.

"What now?" Tristan asked. "Back to the dungeon to be discovered as the old man wants?"

"We won't give him the satisfaction. Let's go to the treasure cave. We can sleep and then watch the sun rise over the sea, a very pretty sight to greet our wedding day," Gareth suggested.

They retraced their steps, but avoiding the path to the castle, continued to the trail winding down to the Serpent's Mouth. Tethering their horses in a secluded nook, the couples made their way carefully to the beach. A tide lured high by the full moon had only recently given up beating against the cliff and begun to recede. Staying close to the wall of rock, they made their way across the slippery shingle and through the small gap in the boulders to the cavern which Callie had heard of from her sister but never beheld. The sea water had come close to the smuggled goods but not touched them. Lunar light poured through the porthole opening and glinted off wine bottles and the metal fittings of casks.

"Someone has been here after us. Much of the wine is gone and the chest of china. They replaced the box of coins to cover the entry to the tunnel, too," Clio remarked.

"Probably Oskar fetching the dishes for the wedding breakfast. I notice a case of champagne is gone. No matter how this adventure began, it appears it will end happily." Tristan shifted some of the goods and presented Clio with a small casket. "This came in from France recently, jewels of the old aristocracy sold off cheap. Look inside and see if you can find a ring for our ceremony or any other bauble to please you."

Clio dug her eager hands into the cold mass of tangled necklaces and earrings hung with pearls and gemstones. She fished out a golden tiara inset with small rubies and set it on her head. "Fit for a marchioness," she declared, then frowned. "Which I am not to be."

Callie hugged her. "I shall share everything with you—barring my husband. But, don't you feel odd possibly wearing the jewels of women who might have died on the guillotine?"

"They have no use for them now, and better we have them than Napoleon. Here is the ring to match with one large stone and a circlet of pearls. Red has always been my color. Let's see if we can find a sapphire for you." Clio did find one, though the gem was not as big as the ruby. It was set in a pleasing gold sunburst. Callie did not care. They entrusted their selections to their husbands-to-be to place on their fingers at the upcoming nuptials. Reluctantly, Clio placed the tiara back into the chest.

The excitement began to wear off, and the girls drooped wearily onto the outspread jackets they'd worn and leaned back against one of the chests. "We should rest until dawn," Clio said. "I only regret we will go to the church in our plainest gowns and with our hair undressed."

"You are as beautiful undressed as dressed," her lover said.

Gareth who had not had the pleasure of seeing his own bride completely naked, could only stand by and redden at his brother's comment. However, he managed something better. "We could return to the castle through the kitchen and rouse your maid to pack some things. We will take her along to the chapel and the vicar's wife can provide a chamber for you to change and primp. Would you like that?"

He got a simultaneous yes. "Good, we will fetch her now while you rest. It might take some time, but be patient. We will return as quickly as we can."

With no chaperones to stop them, they indulged in extravagant farewell kisses, though Clio and Tristan's lasted longer. As soon as the men cleared the cave to go on their errand, she whispered, "I find marital duties far better than mere kisses, not duties at all, really."

Callie rested her head against her sister's shoulder and nodded. "True, so very true." They settled and closed their eyes. How much time passed, they had no idea when voices awakened them. "Our men return," Clio said, but Callie shook her head.

"No, the voices are wrong, rough, older, without education." They rose to meet the unexpected visitors who complained before the entrance to the cave.

"So, you're telling me we had to row against the tide to deliver Captain Digby's bribe. On a night like this, it's a wonder we weren't fired on from the tower. I can't see why his lordship don't pay it out of his own goods. We give him a mighty share."

"Digby's men know enough to turn their backs. As for the rest, Blackwater can have us hung easily as a snap of his lordly fingers for what we do. He'll give back a share when the jewels are sold. He got the connections and will get a better price than the likes of us, Alfie, so shut your gob and roll that barrel in here."

Two thuds sounded against the ground. A cask appeared driven by the hairy, tattooed arms of a seaman bent double to enter the cave. As he straightened, he stopped dead and stared at the two young ladies in white.

"Move on, Alfie. You think I want to spend any more time bent over smelling your arse?"

The first smuggler moved aside, making way for another cask and his partner. "Looks like his lordship left us something to take away, Barney. I heard he brought a whole carriage full of young women to the castle, but I thought they was fine ladies. Guess they must have been your better class of whores like what they got in the city. That old one serves as their madam, then. Mother Grubbs was none too pleased when she told me about the competition for his lordship's business. I suppose she had it pegged right."

"They still look mighty fresh to me, Alf. Hard to believe he used them up so fast, but then there is two more. And do you see—a matched pair as alike as twin wooly lambs? Shipped out and sold to the heathen Musselmen, they'll bring a pretty price, but no reason we can't have a taste of what a pasha has nightly before they go."

Clio and Callie pressed hard together as the smugglers studied them and wrote them off as prostitutes to be sold abroad into the harems of the east. Their own mother and eldest sister had faced such a fate, but being held for ransom, were treated with respect and even privilege. Worth a try with these men, also.

Clio squared her small shoulders. "We are the daughters of the mighty Duke of Bellevue who will reward you well for letting us be. Today we wed Gareth and Tristan Hardacre and will soon be your honored ladies."

The seamen glanced at each other, rubbed their stubbled chins and laughed heartily as if they'd just heard a good joke in a tavern. The burlier of the two swept off his striped stocking cap, releasing greasy gray locks and bowed over it. "Oh, forgive us for not recognizing you, your ladyships. It's rare we see such fine specimens of womanhood, but neither Alfie nor me ever seen a duke's daughter with her hair all a tumble and her garments a mess of wrinkles. Be you actresses in naughty plays, then? I understand their lovers line up outside the stage doors."

"A fine speech Barney, almost as fine as theirs, but lacking the high class accent they put on. Enough talk. I'd like see them perform on their backs. I'll take the one of the right." Alf moved forward. Clio raised her skirts.

"That's a good welcome, then," he said, leering until he saw the sharp blade in her hand.

Equally distracted by the raising of Callie's petticoat, Barney received the same surprise. The twins took a sideways stance, their backs pressed together, their knife hands held close to their bodies until the time came for striking out as dear Papa had taught them.

"Have you ever seen the like—little girlies with big knives," Alfie said, impressed.

"Some of Mother Grubbs' slatterns keep weapons under the mattress, but I never knew one to challenge a customer. Easy enough to take a weapon from such bitty things."

The sailors moved forward in tandem, arms outstretched to seize the blades. Dainty wrists lashed out and left each with a bleeding cut on the forearm. "Blast them both to hell!" Barney roared. "Circle round, Alf."

But the twins had a solid wall of smuggled cargo behind them. They pressed back to back. Their small, lightning jabs opened cuts on the scalps of their assailants that rained down blood into their eyes, another valuable Longleigh lesson.

"Damn it all, I'll shoot them dead if my powder is still dry," Barney declared as he mopped his brow with the stocking cap he'd shoved in his belt a moment ago after mocking them. He pulled it over the wound to staunch the flow of blood, exchanging it for a pistol, but Alfie shoved the gun aside.

"Guess this is why his lordship tired of them. Too much fight for the old man. Can't kill them, Barney. These be prime goods. What say we go back to the boat and get a net and bigger knives than theirs. We snare them, bind them up, and take them to the ship for transport." He flicked a forelock of bloody hair out of his eyes.

"They'll run."

"Where to? How far can they get with the tide still high and the path apiece away? They'll keep until we get back." Prudently, the smugglers backed from the cave rather than risk a knife in the back. Shortly, the girls heard the lap of oars against water.

"Quickly," Clio whispered. "Help me shift the box in front of the bolt hole."

"Will we fit?" Callie questioned even as she shoved at the heavy chest from her end. Clio did the same until it crashed to the floor of the cave and scattered its golden contents across the floor.

"We had better. They are too large to follow us."

"And if they race around and meet us at the other side?"

"They must climb the cliff, then go down the castle's path, very roundabout," Clio answered even as she scrambled onto the top of another box raising her to the level of the hole in the rear of the cavern. She gave her sister a hand. "After you, Marchioness."

"Don't be silly. This is your idea. You go first as ever."

"No time to argue."

She wiggled into the bolt hole. The fit was tight, the dank walls pressing against her shoulders. Nothing but darkness lay ahead. Clio crawled awkwardly with her skirts getting in the way every inch. She wished she'd thought to cut them off with her stiletto now back in its sheath. Behind her, Callie panted with fear, but they progressed, the tunnel gradually widening but entirely straight with no twists or turns to get them lost. Creatures of the dark scuttled before them. Clio gasped as she put her hand on something soft and slimy. Equally repelled, it slithered away. Her hose tore and her knees grew raw, but Callie pressed on behind her murmuring encouraging words.

"I am sure we are almost to the end." Always the sweet optimist, how could she know?

Still, the sound of the surf receded to be replaced by a whiff of marsh and the more domestic sounds of a dog's bark and the cry of a baby in the night. Moonlight made ragged by the shadows of bushes penetrated the shaft. Clio moved forward until she could part those leafy branches. A short drop of a couple of feet proved to be no problem, though she made another rent in her gown when it caught on a twig. Callie tumbled after her. Both wiped their grimy hands on their skirts and smiled their identical smiles.

"Should we try to get back to the castle?" Clio asked her sister.

"I think not. We might run afoul of the smugglers. I think we should take refuge with a kind villager and send a message to Gareth and Tristan to come for us."

"Barely a light in the town except for the back of the house over there. Shall we go around to the front?"

"No, we might be seen from the road!"

They approached cautiously, but no guard dogs assailed them. Clio rapped cautiously at the rear door. At first, no one came, but she persisted. Much to her surprise, a Negro serving woman answered. "We is closing down for the night," she said before she fully took in the sight of identical young ladies in tattered and besmirched white muslin gowns standing on her doorstep.

"We need to see your mistress at once," Clio insisted.

"If you in trouble, maybe you should go see the vicar and not come in here."

"We will be seeing him at eight, but for the moment need your help now," Callie pled.

"Oh, you don't need my help. This Mother Grubbs' house. She'd want a pair like you. You better get on and not come back here."

"Mother Grubbs is the kind lady who took in Gareth and Tristan when they were boys hiding from their father. We should be safe here," Callie confided.

The woman's large eyes rolled in her dark face. "She did take them in, yes, she did."

A harsh voice barked from the interior of the house. "Iola, tell the clients we are closed and shut that door. You'll let in the swamp fever."

"Ain't no clients, Mother. This be two young women you gots to see."

"Looking for work?"

"Say they looking for help."

"I don't run a charity. The women who come here earn their way." As the conversation went on, the rough voice grew closer until the person possessing it stood directly behind her servant. She towered over the rounder, broader Iola, a giantess of a woman topped with brilliant red ringlets held in place with a tiara very similar to the one Clio had coveted in the cave. She appeared to be dressed rather tastelessly for a ball with a low green satin gown showing a great deal of sagging but impressive bosom. Face paint provided her with cherry lips and rosy cheeks and white skin but failed to obscure the deep lines about her mouth and eyes. Those piercing eyes, nearly black, took in every inch of her unexpected guests.

"More discards from the castle, I see. Usually, it's country girls too despoiled to return home that his lordship drops off himself to have handy for later. I can turn most of them into right good whores or out they go. So, Lord Blackwater tired of his city women quickly, and him having sent his boys off to London fetch them."

Callie raised her head and protested. "He did no such thing! We are to marry his sons."

The woman's coarse laughter set her entire bosom to quivering like two blancmange puddings on a plate. "Then do step inside, your ladyships." She made a wide gesture that swept them into a well-lit hallway with many closed doors on either side. "Lock the door, Iola." The servant both shot a bolt and turned a key from one of a bunch that hung at her waist.

Mother Grubbs assessed the girls again with a smirk on her ruby lips. "Pretty, but not bright. You believed that old ploy, did you? Many a maiden has fallen for it before and ended up here."

"Gareth and Tristan will come for us if only you send for them. Then you'll see." Clio said.

"Ah, those two warm puppies. I taught them all they should know of bedding a woman—at the same time. Quite enough of me to share, so their father always said. What a treat they were! The two of you still virgins—as if that's likely after a stay at the castle?"

"Until very recently," Callie admitted with the deepest blush her dark complexion could muster before Clio could cut her off with a "None of your concern!"

"I don't take virgins into my house. But if you've only been debauched recently, you'll take some training. I am thinking I can charge more than double for a tandem team. Iola, bring wash water and soap. See if Maizie might have dressing gowns to fit such paltry little creatures. They'd drown in mine. I'll send to the castle and see if Blackwater is done with them once he has slept off his nightly stupor. You must have displeased him mightily for him to toss you out in such a state, all grubby and tattered."

"We didn't please him, not one bit!" Clio declared with hands on hips.

"We pleased our husbands-to-be," Callie insisted.

"Maybe they will want to keep you here exclusively. Most likely their old man threw you out from jealousy because they would not share." Mother Grubbs stroked her long chin thoughtfully. A bit of her face paint came off on her fingertips. "There are those who prefer only to watch and a foursome would loosen their purses."

Clio stiffened. "I believe we have come to the wrong place for assistance. Our mistake. We shall go elsewhere. Come, sister."

They turned toward the locked door expecting Iola to open it before them as servants always did, but this woman was not in their employ. She remained a solid, black lump standing in front of it. From behind, the towering Mother Grubbs seized them, one under each arm and hauled them away kicking and screaming loud enough to wake the dead or at least dozing prostitutes. Doors opened in the corridor and irritated whores demanded to know who disturbed their rest.

"New recruits. Go back to sleep, ladies. They will quiet soon enough even if I have to bind their mouths." She carried the twins past a small chamber where the nightly take still sat on a desk built to suit the madame's size taking up most of the space. Candlelight glinted off the stacks of coins. Mother Grubbs started up a staircase with a nicely polished railing and a parlor off to one side as decently furnished as in many a fine home.

Another black servant sitting in a chair by the front door rose to offer his help. He wore a white wig and a golden livery gaudier than the one Oskar had been forced to don. In size, he rivaled Mother Grubbs, but had considerably more muscle. "Do you need my assistance, madam?"

"No, Roscoe, they weigh no more than a goodly sack of flour, but if they do not stop squirming, I will turn them over to you." The girls went limp in her arms.

"There now, that's better. March ahead and none of us need worry about a spill down the stairs. Keep those tiny mouths shut, too. You are noisier than nestling birds. My women need their rest. The Hawkhurst gang divided their shares tonight, and they will be back tomorrow to play some more."

With the threatening Roscoe at the base of the stairs and Mother Grubbs right behind, the twins had no choice but to travel meekly upward, then down a hallway to a room on the far end. "I call this my training chamber, much like those fancy gymnasiums young men of quality like to favor, but here we prepare for a different kind of sport. Enter. It is quite comfortable." She took a candle burning in a wall sconce and lit two oil lamps on either side of a bed large enough for two—or four. Only one small, high, barred window pierced the wall.

Iola came in shortly, a bucket of steaming water hanging from one hand and a pair of silken dressing gowns thrown over the other arm. Setting down a hairbrush on the washstand, she filled a china basin with the water and offered the twins the wrappers, thin and fanciful with decorations of bright birds and overblown roses, and of such a small size as to leave much of the body revealed.

"Maizie want to know what's in this for her," Iola said as she handed over the gowns to the twins.

"Why, new dressing gowns and perhaps a frock. We shall see. As for you, my fresh girls, disrobe and wash. Hot water is always at the ready. You have only to ring for it. You will have all your customers wash their privates before getting into bed, and you will learn to check them for disease. You shall wash yours after each client. I do pride myself that I run the finest establishment in the marshes, thanks to Blackwater's patronage. I feel my place rivals any found in London town. If you require help undressing, Iola will stay and assist you. For a slave, she is well-trained."

"No, we disapprove of slavery and can't in good conscience accept her assistance," Clio said at once.

"We can aid each other," Callie added. "We always have."

"Suit yourselves. Yes, once you settle in, you will be quite the novelty. Iola, lock the door and go to your rest."

Left alone, the twins pondered their situation. "At least, they have not discovered our weapons. We might as well wash and use the dressing gowns. I'd hate to have Gareth see me in such a state," Callie said with a sigh. The room offered plenty of mirrors, one over the washstand, another full-length on a wall and a third above the bed taking the place of a canopy. All attested to their woeful condition.

"Then we will be in no condition to flee, though we could bathe and dress again. If we summon Iola to bring more hot water, we might threaten her with our knives and make our escape." Acting on her words, Clio turned to let her sister unfasten her gown and raise it over her head. Undergarments followed until she sat on the side of the bed in nothing but her shredded silk stockings and the leg sheath holding her stiletto. The stockings she shucked and tossed away, then provided the same service for Callie. Both stowed their stilettos under the rather nice feather pillows the better to get at them quickly.

"Getting by the monstrous footman who guards the locked door and past Mother Grubbs whom I suspect is still up counting her ill-gotten gains—I think it unlikely. This is precisely the kind of place we aren't supposed to know about, but do now firsthand, the kind of place James took our young men in London. I admit I did not recognize it from the rear and in the darkness, a grave error on our part." Callie sighed as she washed the smut from her face and the blood from her abraded knees. Running the washcloth between her thighs, she still caught the slight scent of roses. "Do you think Gareth and Tristan really did deceive us?"

"Nonsense!" Clio declared in a voice that sounded very much like their mother. "Even if they did not want us, we have twenty-thousand pounds each to bring to a union. No one throws that kind of fortune away. They will marry us."

"Not very romantic, but practical, I suppose. In my heart, I know they will come for us soon."

They took turns at brushing their always problematic curls, neither wanting to put on their badly soiled clothes nor wishing to wear a whore's borrowed dressing gowns. Their bodies were the same and no novelty to them no matter how often reflected in the mirrors. "We should lie down and rest to be better prepared to meet whoever comes through that door in the morning," Clio said.

Nude, they curled into the featherbed, exhausted, and slept.

Twenty-four

The powerful blows on the green door brought the vicar to his window again. With his nightcap nearly falling off, he leaned over the sill. "There is supposed to be no rest for the wicked, not the godly. What is it now? Ah, a new pair has found their way to my home, the marquess' minion and another. Who might you be to come knocking at such an hour?"

With a minimal bow of his head, James replied, "Viscount Laughlin, seeking his twin sisters so scurrilously abducted by the Hardacre boys."

"You are rather roughly dressed for a lord, out at the elbows, but your accent and your arrogance tell me it might be so."

A man taller than most and riding a horse meant to accommodate his long legs, James rose up in his stirrups and drew his slim sword. Raised at arm's length, he pressed it against the vicar's soft throat. "Do you have my sisters within?"

"No, indeed! They are to return at eight as agreed to be married. The marquess has no intention of allowing two heiresses to slip through his hands, so you needn't worry about their reputations. As a man of the cloth, I can keep a secret—though a suitable donation to a poor church would be welcome."

James observed the fat accumulated under the vicar's chin and felt if the church were poor, its coffers had been emptied to feed the man. "Something might be arranged once I find my sisters. Have you any idea where they are?"

"None, but they will be here at eight. Return then." The vicar retreated from the tip of the sword and shut the window with such force the panes rattled in their frames.

"Back to the castle, then, where I will skewer the livers of those young men if any harm has come to Clio and Callie."

James turned his horse as Oskar tried a few placating words. "Now, now, all will be well. Ye shall see.

~ * ~

"Damnation! Who barred the kitchen door?" Tristan swore.

"Probably Oskar awoke and believed he'd neglected his duty. Knock and rouse him," Gareth suggested reasonably.

Tristan did far more than that. He added a few kicks of his boot against the heavy wood of the portal. Oskar did not answer his summons. Instead, someone struggled to lift the substantial bar and called out, "Patience!" The bar fell with a thud and Finch, dressed in her uniform and ready for whatever service she was called upon to provide, stood in the doorway. "Here you are, but where are my babies?"

"Safe, but they want you to come to them and bedeck them for their wedding this morning," Gareth explained.

"Easier done if you had brought them here," the maid answered with exasperation.

"We mean to keep them from embarrassment. Come, we will use the secret stairs to regain their chamber and pack all you shall need." Gareth shooed her toward the fireplace and the hidden stairs.

"I see young men have no idea of the extent of a woman's needs on her wedding day. Regardless, I shall give it my best try." Finch took up a candle and followed them into the dark maw of the staircase.

They came out from behind the arras to find both beds occupied. "Ah, my dear lambs have come back all on their own. However did this bed get broken?" Finch exclaimed, and gently shook the shoulder of the nearest sleeping form ensconced on a mattress resting nearly on the floor amidst a welter of bedclothes forming a cocoon around its occupant. Clarissa Downey bolted upright from her rest. Finch jumped back. "What are you doing in my girl's bed?"

"Resting from the trials of seduction and elopement, I thought. Not mine, but the twins' escapade. James has gone to find them." She eyed the Hardacre boys. "He is very unhappy with the two of you. We escaped from our own chamber through that trapdoor above but were unable to climb back into it and thought to remain here until morning."

Her voice awoke Lady Mallet who had claimed the intact bed by reason of rank and age. Releasing the still sleeping Angelique from her grasp, she, too, sat up and grumbled, "Whether we are to have a nuptial celebration or a duel to the death in a few hours, I shall not be able to enjoy it unless well rested." Her daughter began to stir. "Stay under the covers, dearest. Young men have invaded our place. If they see you indecent, one or the other must marry you."

"Not that again," Clarissa said. "Do by all means stay hidden, Angelique. I am sure Lord Blandon will take you if he cannot have one of Bellevue's twins." Addressing the Hardacres she continued. "What exactly are you doing here? I thought you'd run off to be wed."

Shamefaced and staring at his boot tips in the presence of so many ladies abed, Gareth answered, "We came to retrieve clean gowns for the wedding ceremony in a few hours."

"Oh, we shall need much more than that," Finch assured him. She began to open boxes, emptying the contents out of a small camelback trunk and refilling it with clean undergarments, stockings and two pair of kid slippers. She held up matching dresses, one of pale pink with a lace overlay and the other of blue similarly ornamented. "What do you think of these as wedding garments?" she asked her audience.

"Suitable," said Lady Mallet.

"Charming," Clarissa replied.

Angelique exposed one blue eye and commented, "I wish I had a gown so pretty."

Into the small trunk the dresses went along with sashes and ribbons and necklaces and hair ornaments and gloves. She added hairbrushes and toiletries, finally topping it off with two hatboxes containing matching chapeaux. "There we are. Now, where do we find my ladies?"

"In the sea cave beneath the cliff," Tristan confessed.

"A sea cave! Well, you will simply have to carry them across the beach once they are dressed and then directly to the vicar before their gowns become dirtied again."

"We are entirely willing to do that," Gareth said. "Ladies, return to your dreams."

He hefted one side of the chest and Tristan took the other. They made their way awkwardly down the narrow staircase with Finch lighting their way. Continuing on through the kitchen, they passed out of the castle's permanently open portcullis, down the precarious path to the shingle below with Finch hugging close to the wall of the cliff every step of the way. Glad of the retreating tide, they crossed the moonlit beach though the beams from that orb began to fade as dawn approached. The men lifted the trunk high to get it through the narrow aperture leading to the cave and shoved it before them into the low entrance.

"Here we are, darlings, with Finch and your wedding clothes," Gareth proclaimed as he straightened only to stare into the faces of two of his father's favorite smugglers. "What have you done with the young women we left here?"

One clutched a fishing net to his chest. The other had a brace of cutlasses shoved through his belt. Both appeared somewhat bloodied. Barney Ludlum pulled off a stocking cap and reopened a clot on his scalp that immediately began to ooze. "Begging your pardon, young lordships, they done more to us than we to them. Quick with knives, they are. Who woulda thought they knew of the passage and had the size and the nerve to pass through it?"

"Oh, Longleigh women seldom wait to be rescued, according to the duchess. They take matters into their own hands," Finch informed them.

"Whatever you call them, gone they were when we came back to subdue them light skirts and carry them off to the Near East as we believed the marquess intended. Never fear, we'll find those little whores and get a good price for them, too, in the end."

Tristan Hardacre's fist met Barney's jaw. The seaman crumpled, tangled like a cod in his own net. Alf attempted to draw a cutlass but had it only halfway out when he succumbed to an equal blow from Gareth. "Do not dare to speak of our brides that way!"

For good measure, Finch kicked each in the ribs with her small pointed shoe. Prudently, both men stayed down.

"Didn't touch a hair on their curly heads nor elsewhere neither," Alf said in his own defense.

"A misunderstandin' then, your lordships. We wish you all happiness," Barney offered from his place on the cave floor.

The twins exchanged glances. "We both know where the tunnel comes out," said Gareth.

"To Mother Grubbs' house, then," Tristan agreed.

"I pray this Mother Grubbs has taken good care of my ladies," Finch said.

"She had better," Gareth assured her. He shoved the wedding chest through the cave entrance again and picked up his end. Tristan and Finch followed to assay the cliff path once more.

Twenty-five

Bristol arrived to light the ovens for the daily bread and found the kitchen entry carelessly unbarred. Usually, he knocked until Oskar rolled from his blankets to let him inside, but neither Oskar nor the maid newly come to the castle appeared to be present. The turnspit dogs did greet him as he usually fed them their bowls of scraps at this hour before letting them out to do their business in the courtyard. No concern of his...he had loaves to prepare, more and fancier than usual as the marquess said a wedding was in the works. Not his to question the master though no banns had been read in the local church.

After he'd heated the ovens and prepared the dough, some with swirls of cinnamon and dots of raisins, others pinched into plain rolls or coiled up like snail shells to be adorned with icing and candied fruit, he sat to await the second rising and have a mug of cider with the remains of yesterday's bread and a good dollop of butter accompanied by sheep's milk cheese. A pounding on the door interrupted his repast. Rising, he found Mother Grubbs' darkling manservant waiting with a missive from that same lady for the marquess. She hadn't bothered to seal the message hastily written in big, bold script much like the woman herself. Probably figured no one at the castle could read other than the marquess and his sons, but Bristol had found it handy to learn and put his knowledge to work discovering new recipes even if finer cookery was seldom called for at Castle Blackwater. As soon as the black giant left, he took a quick glance. Special knowledge always came in handy.

> My Dearest Lordship—
>
> I have at my house your twin discards. Are they to be kept for your especial use or might they be trained to accept my general clientele? I believe you would enjoy watching them perform. Both claim they are no longer virgins and knowing your prowess, I believe them.
>
> Ever at your Service—
> Maida Grubbs

Bristol's brows shot up to his close-cropped hairline. The way Oskar and Finch doted on those girls, he'd assumed them to be the finest of ladies, but what did he know of London society? He did not tarry but carried the note to the great hall of the castle and nudged aside the pile of dogs that covered his master.

"Awake, your lordship. A message of importance has arrived from Mother Grubbs." While Bristol did not touch the man, his deep voice filled the void of the hall and finally penetrated the ears of the marquess. The man woke still mostly dressed and covered in the hair of his hounds. After scratching his head to rid himself of a few stray fleas, he snatched the letter and applied his bloodshot eyes to the page.

"Ah, my sons followed my orders but evidently found the young women lacking and dumped them at the brothel. Or perhaps the fault lay with them as they were reluctant. Regardless, they must marry the chits for their fortunes unless they have decided upon the blonde and the near titless wench with the skinny hips, though I can't imagine why. As the twin girls are no longer virgins, I believe I am free to sample their wares. If one pleases me, I'll have her to wife and leave the other to be my mistress since the boys are done with them. Continue with the wedding feast, Cookie. Someone shall marry today, and it might be me."

"As you wish, milord." Bristol returned to his tasks. He had buns to put in the oven, and at the break of day, the village women would arrive to assist in preparing the elaborate breakfast. Over the years, he'd seen and heard worse within the castle. At least one of the young ladies would come out of this a bride, though a miserable one to be sure if wedded to the Marquess of Blackwater.

~ * ~

James Longleigh rode slowly back to the castle. His keen gray eyes searched every nook of the small town for some sign of his errant sisters. He found nothing. As they approached the brothel sitting like a bunion on the foot of the castle's hill, Oskar frowned.

"That's his lordship's mount tied out front. Strange time o' the day to be satisfying the cravings of the flesh with dawn nearly upon us. Mother Grubbs keeps strict hours, though she'd bend the rules for Lord Blackwater."

Well aware of the services offered from the suggestions made by the women hanging in the windows upon their arrival, something niggled at James. "We should look within for my sisters."

"My boys would never leave them in such a place!" the outraged Oskar declared. "Besides, we'd have to get by her manservant, a great black beast who keeps a cudgel by the door to handle anyone denied entry and is equally good at tossing outside those who offend."

"While I believe we could handle him, a stealthy approach might be more prudent. Is there a back entrance?"

"To be sure. At times, the redcoats come down from their tower to take their pleasure and the smugglers must make their exit quickly out the rear."

Leaving their horses tied beside Blackwater's steed, they moved quietly behind the building. As a lad, James had enjoyed learning Shawnee woodcraft from his father on the estate of Bellevue Hall, but as he grew he disdained his savage training. Still, the skills never left him. He immediately sighted a broken bush bearing a scrap of white cloth as the early rays of dawn began to light the area. Rubbing the fabric between his fingertips, he knew it to be of good quality. As children, his sisters had constantly snagged their clothing acting outrageously for little girls. Their father laughed, commending them on their spirit. Where had that spirit placed them now? In a bordello, from the looks of two sets of small footprints in the damp earth heading toward the house of ill repute.

"My sisters are inside," he pronounced.

Oskar differed. "I don't believe it. Gently bred girls would never enter a place so foul."

"Gently bred girls would not know a haven from a hell hole even if they are hellions themselves. If I stay in the shadows, can you get someone to open the rear door for you?"

Oskar shrugged his big shoulders. "I know the maid, Iola. More than once I've been summoned to bear his lordship home from this place when in his cups."

"Try her, then."

James flattened himself against a wall near the stoop while Oskar rapped. His noise did bring Iola, complaining and sleepy-eyed. "Me, I get no rest this evening. Always someone banging on this door—some girls, Lord Blackwater, now you, Oskar. What you want at this hour?"

James pushed by her bulk. "Those girls, where are they?"

"You can't go up there. Lord Blackwater is wit' them."

"They are my sisters. I've come to save them from an awful fate."

"Roscoe and me, we be owned by Mother Grubbs. If we tell anything what goes on here, we get a beating, or maybe sold off to a worse place."

"Slavery, how I loathe it!" James gave her that compelling gray-eyed stare he'd inherited from his mother. He knew its effect. "Would you condemn two innocents to another type of bondage?"

Iola's big brown bosom rose and fell with a great sigh. "Tell Roscoe you have come to sample the new wares along with the marquess. Second floor, end room on the right. Oskar, fetch me a good clout to the face so I can say you beat this out of me."

"Brace yourself, Iola." He drew back his fist and sent the slave woman sprawling on her broad backside with a blow that would surely bruise a cheek and close one eye. "Sorry, pet."

Oskar led the way to the staircase before the servant had a chance to cup her face and mumble her thanks. Roscoe leapt to his feet from his chair by the front door. He overtopped even James Longleigh and possessed an impressive breadth of muscle. "What goes on in the kitchen?"

"Iola took a tumble. You should see to her," Oskar said.

"We've come to help the marquess break in the new girls," James added to justify their presence. He took the stairs without pausing.

"Eager man," Roscoe commented, as if he'd seen plenty of the type.

"Who wouldn't be? Maybe we'll go next if Mother sees fit," Oskar replied with a wink of his one good eye as he followed Lord Laughlin.

At the far end of the hall, a door stood open. Mother Grubbs, her back turned to them, blocked the way. James removed her with a sharp jerk to the elbow that spun the woman round despite her great size. What he beheld in that chamber, he hoped never to see again. His sisters stood naked as Venus on her half shell, but considerably better armed, each with her stiletto in hand as they faced Lord Blackwater. Their black curls tumbled over tawny breasts peaked with the early morning chill. He wanted to close his eyes against viewing the dark patch between their legs and their shapely limbs, but that would be most inadvisable considering the marquess stood confronting them with trousers unbuttoned exposing an erection nearly as impressive as the saber in his hand.

"Come to join the fun?" Blackwater said, instantly turning and swiping at James with his blade.

James leapt back and fluidly drew his epee. "Foul pig, you die today!"

"Or you," the marquess countered. However, his tumescence deflated when Laughlin nicked it with the very tip of his sword as it slipped beneath his guard. He was not prepared for an attack on his unguarded rear by the two savage girls with their knives held high to stab. Only a warning from Mother Grubbs saved him. "Behind you!" Blackwater swiveled to confront all three. He used wide sweeps of his saber to keep them at bay.

"Do not make me mar your pretty hides," he threatened the twins.

If he thought to rattle them, he failed. They held their weapons low, looking for an opening to jab at him. James, with his longer reach and lengthy sword, tormented him, worrying his exposed privates, and when he sought to guard them, swooping in to pierce a shoulder. Forced to circle, he came up against the wide bed and mounted it by the bed steps. An old dog, but a sly one, with a slash he cut the bed curtains free to entangle his opponents and with a leap made for the doorway. Mother Grubbs shouted for Roscoe to bring his cudgel as Oskar held her back from joining the brawl on Lord Blackwater's side.

James should have known the marquess would be no easy man to kill. Kicking away the drapes, he ordered, "Stay here, sisters! Cover yourselves." By the patter of small, bare footsteps behind him, he knew the twins had disobeyed again, only giving him more cause to worry. He pursued the man down the hallway where bleary-eyed whores peered from half-open doors. But the coming of huge Roscoe blocked Blackwater's way to the stairs and forced him into the alcove providing light to the second story with its remarkable stained-glass window. The languorous nereids regarded the battle with no interest at all in their blank eyes.

James soon had Blackwater pinned against the fragile glass, though the man continued to flail at him. His disobedient sisters saved his life. "Down," they shouted. He ducked without questioning. The mighty cudgel wielded by Roscoe missed his skull, creating a breeze as it passed and barely avoided braining Lord Blackwater. It did, however, shatter the lovely sea nymphs all to bits. Cracks formed like circles in a pond radiating through their long hair and lush bodies. Shards of colored glass rained on the cobbles below. The marquess lowered his guard as he felt his backing give way. James lunged forward to strike a fatal blow but could not complete his mission as Blackwater fell from the window. Two small warm bodies pressed closed behind him as all three stared at the street below where the Marquess of Blackwater lay atop a camelback chest carried by his two sons.

"Never fear, Lord Laughlin, I got a hold on Roscoe," Oskar announced behind them. Rather than struggle, the massive slave fell to his knees before the outraged Mother Grubbs. "Madam, forgive me for breaking your fine window."

"And killing my best patron. You will pay for both when I sell you off to work on a sugar plantation in the Indies."

"That is very unfair," said Clio with her hands on her naked hips like an outraged sylph. "He only did as you bid him. The blow went wrong because we cried out."

"Yes, my family has strong objections to slavery. When I am marchioness, I will not allow it in my domain," Callie asserted. "In fact, I shall buy both of your Negroes from you and free them."

Mother Grubbs shook her head, her red locks snaking Medusa-like from her disheveled coiffure. "A pity about the two of you. You have the boldness to do well in the trade. Give me what I ask, and they are yours."

Heavy boots charged up the stairs with a lighter step behind. When the Hardacre twins stopped dead in their tracks upon beholding the scene of the groveling slave, the worse for wear James Longleigh, and their naked brides, Finch pushed between them. "Avert your eyes at once! Go back and fetch the trunk. Come along, my lambs. I think I see an open chamber at the end of the hall where we shall bedeck you as brides. Your wedding hour is not far off."

"But isn't it unseemly to hold this wedding when Lord Blackwater lies dead below?" James asked, full of hope at stopping the whole fiasco and returning his sisters more or less intact to London. Surely neither could be pregnant after just one go at it.

"Oh," Finch said. "The chest broke his fall. Lord Blackwater is still very much alive."

James groaned. "Then I must try to kill him again."

"No!" the twins answered in unison as Finch, shielding them with her skirts held wide, herded them toward the bedchamber. "Thanks to your intervention, brother, he never touched us," Callie stated.

"I believe we could have defeated him by ourselves," Clio, the ever-confident, said. "However, you cannot kill a man simply for evil intentions never carried out."

"Yes, I can," James assured them.

"Well, it is our wedding day. Allow our future father-in-law to live as a gift to us," Callie suggested.

"Have it your own way, then, but when we return to London, I will say I saw only your magnificence in battle and nothing more. Nothing—more." Their giggles as the bedchamber door closed only added to James Longleigh's embarrassment.

Twenty-six

Lord Blackwater appeared too wobbly to sit his horse. Though the chest of wedding finery had saved his ill-lived life, he'd hit his head with such force that the camel back had cracked in the middle. Once his woody pillow was removed by his sons who delivered it to the second floor of the bawdyhouse, he had difficulty standing without Oskar's assistance.

James Longleigh sneered at the marquess' sad condition. "As you are in no shape to continue our duel in all fairness, I shall return to the castle and summon a carriage for your transport.

Unable to reach his saber lying several feet away, Blackwater replied, "Any time, any place, anywhere, you arrogant prig."

James declined to answer, but merely mounted and set off on the steep trail to the castle. He returned in good time with the conveyance that performed a double task. Once Blackwater had been buttoned up and returned, the ladies of their party came aboard to witness the wedding. Oh, they did complain of the early hour and the inadequacy of their dress since Finch had been unavailable to help them. However, curiosity overrode having to tie each other sashes and mend their coiffures with hairpins as well as they were able. Bonnets covered most of the improvisations.

Again, doxies sat in the windows of Mother Grubbs' establishment as the two brides, rather brown for nobility, but radiant just the same, left the whorehouse for a life those inside would never know. In their silks and laces, their black curls twined with artificial rosebuds, their small hands clasped together, the twins trod carefully over the broken glass nymphs. Their brother, washed, shaved, and refurbished as well, helped them into the carriage. A few bitter sighs sent them on their way, though one whore bolder than the rest cried, "Still half price for you, lovely gentleman!"

James ignored the offer for now. He had to admit his sisters cleaned up well and even brought a lump to his throat as they toddled side by side down the short aisle toward the vicar finally out of his nightshirt and placated by an invitation to the wedding breakfast for his lost sleep. Still, he did not envy the eager grooms, dressed to London standards under his tutelage. Those rosebud mouths would have the Hardacre boys trained to jump through hoops like circus puppies in no time. No marriage for James Longleigh, at least not for ages.

Upon return to the castle, the wedding party found the marquess had unpacked his ostentatious bejeweled goblets and golden chargers again, though they were topped with fine French china pieces, all matching now. Bristol had outdone himself in preparing a feast fit for a better man than his master, and excellent champagne was not stinted in the least. Lady Mallet cautioned her charges, "Sip slowly and eat often lest you become inebriated like our host."

Indeed, when the marquess, his head sheathed in white bandages making him appear like an oriental potentate, rose to propose a toast, he slumped badly to one side and slurred his words. "To my shuns— may they share what they brought into our family."

James jumped to his feet, hand on the hilt of the sword he should have rightly left in his chamber to avoid the temptation to use it. He received a crooked smile from Blackwater who continued, "By which I mean their dowries." The marquess drained his goblet even though some of the wine dribbled from the side of his mouth. "Oskar, more champagne for my damnable headache."

Lady Mallet stiffened at his language. "Drunken sot," she muttered.

Oskar refilled the goblet halfway only to be chided by his master for a full draught. "More, you villain!" The servant complied. Phineas Hardacre, Marquess of Blackwater, took a great swallow, gagged, dropped his cup, and sank beneath the table.

"Disgusting," remarked Lady Mallet. "But now we can enjoy ourselves at leisure."

Oskar dragged his master from beneath the table linens and knelt by his lord's side. The evil eyes held no light and stared blankly at the vaulted ceiling. The foul mouth hung open. Oskar pressed a hand to the unmoving chest. "Milords and ladies, I believe the marquess is dead."

"Divine justice," Lady Mallet said quite clearly while her daughter covered her face in distress. She helped herself to another of the delightful iced buns.

"How very gothic to die at a wedding feast," Clarissa Downey remarked.

The Hardacre boys went to their father's side, but relief more than grief showed clearly on their features. They helped Oskar carry the man from the great hall with the vicar, a tad tipsy himself, following to recite the words for the dying or in this case, the dead.

The two young brides stared at each other, mirror images, though perhaps Callie's face was softer. Still, they shed no tears for their lost father-in-law. "Now you are a marchioness," Clio said. "I will always to be your inferior."

"Never," Callie answered her.

~ * ~

James stayed on for the funeral to assist in any way he could for the sake of his newly married sisters. Both wore black as Finch had hastily dyed two white muslin gowns for the occasion. Without their colored sashes and ribbons, he couldn't have told them apart were it not for the ruby and sapphire rings on their fingers. Laid out in his own hall, Lord Blackwater received final visitations from the citizenry of Marston who wanted to make sure of his death before secretly rejoicing, and by his partners in smuggling who took the new marquess aside to see if their agreement with the old lord still held. James assumed by the nodding of their heads it did. Nobles were few in the marshes, and Blackwater had befriended none of them to mourn for him.

Captain Thornton from the Martello tower arrived in a resplendent dress uniform and spent a great deal of time at Angelique's side as if she were a grieving relative he needed to comfort. "So terrible," she whimpered, dabbing at her watery blue eyes. "He had a fall from his horse on an early morning ride and later died right before our eyes at the wedding breakfast." She dutifully repeated the lie she'd been told.

"I am here to offer you comfort and assist you in any way that I can," the captain assured her with a bold smile quickly suppressed. "Still, you must find the double elopement very romantic. Those truly attracted to each other should let nothing stand in their way, don't you think?" He leaned close allowing his hot breath to whisper against her cheek.

Angelique stepped back. "No, I don't find elopement romantic anymore. I should want a cathedral wedding and a gown made especially for the occasion, a much nicer breakfast without anyone falling dead, to be followed by a wedding trip abroad. That is why I will not linger here a day longer than I must. I need to get back to London and find a proper husband."

James Longleigh, who lingered nearby in case he needed to step in to stop an improper advance, observed the captain make his bow and retreat to the free barrels of ale tapped for the occasion. No need, as Angelique had handled herself very well. The story he had given out about the marquess' death sounded so much better than having the local lord with his private parts exposed fall from a brothel window after attempting to force himself upon his daughters-in-law.

Since the Hardacre boys lacked sufficient eloquence, James had been pressed into service to write the obituary and post it to the London papers. With their guidance, he mentioned Lord Blackwater's distinguished service in the Royal Navy, the name of his deceased wife, and of course his survivors, Gareth Hardacre, Viscount Marston, and his wife, Lady Calliope nee Longleigh, and Lord Tristan Hardacre and his wife, Lady Clio, nee Longleigh. They unanimously agreed on the "fall from a horse" cause of death. He sent the notice posthaste to his parents with a very brief explanatory note describing the marriages as an elopement brought on by a surfeit of ardor on both sides and urged the duke to seek out and send along the special license that languished somewhere in the bureaucracy of the church—if it had ever been applied for in the first place.

Regardless, most of the real witnesses to the true debacle were moving on to another town. Not only had his sisters wheedled the purchase of a pair of slaves to be freed for their wedding gift, they also dictated the closure of the brothel in such close proximity to the castle, thus proving that the best time to ask for favors was while the grooms were still besotted. James supposed he would never claim that half-price offer from the bawd, nor would the Hardacre boys. He had to say his sisters, for all their silliness, did not lack intelligence. As for the Negroes, they labored as servants in the castle keeping the boards groaning with funeral meats.

Callie, laying her sapphire-ringed hand on her brother's arm, explained, "Roscoe has the makings of a magnificent butler and Iola a fine maid. Of course, Oskar will remain as our steward and Finch as our housekeeper. Bristol agrees to continue on as cook and even appears excited by the prospect. He says he has so many recipes he wants to try. And if we decide upon a livery, it will surely *not* be green and orange."

"Once you vacate the alchemist's chamber, we plan to do our writing there," Clio added.

"Writing? Not more gothic horrors!"

"But of course. We live in a castle now, the perfect setting. Our sister Iris used Ira Long as her pseudonym for painting. We have decided on C.C. Leigh."

"As long as you leave my name out of it, do as you will."

Clio gave her brother one of those insidious bow-shaped smiles. "We would never think of using you as our hero. We've decided upon

Lord Jasper Leithmore. The sword fight will take place on the castle staircase as Lord Jasper drives the evil marquess to his death in a plunge off the battlements."

Callie, her cheeks growing dusky pink with excitement, continued, "The two young heroines, Cleoma and Cassandra, will be clothed in diaphanous nightwear for the sake of decency, but both will have their stilettos handy."

"Neither of them shall swoon at any time," Clio stated.

Standing nearby, Clarissa Downey raised an eyebrow. "I've heard worse plots. Will you be escorting us back to London, Lord Leithmore? Sorry, Lord Laughlin."

James gave her a wry smile. "As soon as Blackwater is in the ground. I've had enough of gothic living."

That time came quickly. As the mourners thinned, Phineas Hardacre was boxed in and covered with a black pall. A cart drew him past the brothel he had frequented and on to the church where he rarely attended. The vicar performed the traditional service and consigned Lord Blackwater to the family crypt to lie beside the wife who'd feared and hated him. Ironically, the brother she would have preferred rested on her other side leaving her ever in the middle. Long live the new marquess.

As the ceremony ended, a lathered horse which had not been spared drew up before the church. The rider provided the vicar with a special license handily backdated which legitimized the marriage of the Longleigh twins. Its sudden appearance bespoke of the power and wealth of the Duke of Bellevue to whom his son would soon have to answer.

The carriage less crowded by two left the following morning. James saw all the ladies to their doors. He pressed a book into Angelique's hands. "My sisters wanted you to have this as you hadn't finished reading it." He held out their copy of *The Castle of Otronto*.

"No, thank you, Lord Laughlin. Return it to Bellevue's library. I have found witnessing gothic adventures far more frightful than reading about them. Being locked in a castle tower, running around ill-clothed in drafty corridors, and witnessing the death of a villain at the breakfast table is decidedly dreadful. I wish a more regular life for myself and doubt I would ever have that aligned with the Longleigh family."

James kissed the air above her gloved hand in parting. Despite her protestations, she was not immune enough to his charms to withhold a blush. "Lady Angelique, you are gracious in defeat."

He spoke a few words to Clarissa Downey, too, before leaving. "I've rarely met a young woman of such rare good sense and intellect, my wayward sisters included. I will look for those qualities when I finally decide to marry," he said.

Clarissa did have very good sense for she answered, "I am flattered but do not plan to swoon in your arms. In fact, I am spoken for by a suitor who cares not if I step upon his feet in the dance or wear spectacles. He swears he will never hinder me from reading what I want or discussing what I will. We accept each other as we are, truly a rare case in society marriages. He should have approached my father by now."

"Who is the lucky man?"

"Chester Buckley, brother of Lord Blandon, of course. We will live on the estate in our own wing of the manor house. My only fear is that I might end up with Angelique as my sister-in-law since Chet said his brother is considering her. Evidently, Blandon's attempted seduction of a Longleigh twin went awry." Clarissa cocked her head as if awaiting an explanation.

James immediately turned the subject back to her. He had learned from the best at his mother's table. "Why ever did you go along to Castle Blackwater then?"

Clarissa presented a smile almost as arch as his sisters were capable of creating. "I've heard of the Longleigh family adventures, some of them written down, and now I've been part of one. I do hope I rate a few pages in the twins' book if only for comic relief."

"Then, I wish you all happiness, Miss Downey," he said, bowing low over her hand and breathing the lightest kiss even closer to her flesh than the one he'd presented to Angelique. It truly did make her shiver.

"I wish the same for you when your time comes."

"Not any time soon," he said in parting. His parents awaited and a very long explanation as well.

Twenty-seven

Callie, Clio, and their husbands sat in the alchemist's chamber atop the tower and perused a letter from the Duke and Duchess of Bellevue that was at once a scolding for their dangerous antics and yet a congratulations on their marriages and a wish for their eternal happiness now that they had gained what they desired. Their mother chided them for driving James away once more. After apologizing for his poor ability to curb his sisters and most likely giving a whitewashed account of their adventures, he'd set sail for Egypt now that the French had given up the place. The duchess continued by writing:

No matter how I pled, he would only say we'd have some peace for a few years since his two younger brothers were next in line to enter society and could tend to their own marriage prospects which had to be easier than dealing with any daughter. Exclaiming that after them comes Pandora who is as much trouble as twins but in only one body and his help would be needed, James replied that we would have to find him first. Let his brothers serve as her chaperones.

All four of the readers laughed. The twins sat side by side behind the huge desk where Mother Grubbs had counted her coins. She had been bought out, as the old proverb said, lock, stock and barrel, and transferred with her women to another town to start her business anew. Her fine parlor furnishings now dwelled in a sitting area of the great hall making it much more comfortable and inviting. Fresher furniture would be ordered later. The massive desk and cabinets had been laboriously moved into the tower by Oskar and Roscoe to serve the newly fledged writers. With one girl being right-handed and the other left-handed, they did not disturb each other at all when they wrote.

Callie, her elbows resting on its shining surface and her hands framing her elfin face, said, "I am so deliriously happy I want everyone to marry. I suspect Oskar will ask Finch to be his wife when he can find the courage."

"Do you really think so? I can't imagine them breeding little Finches and great big Oskars," Gareth questioned.

"Yes!" both the Longleigh girls replied.

"Or huge Finches and tiny Oskars," Tristan jested.

"I doubt that will be a problem. I am sure both are well past thirty," Clio said in the all-knowing way of a seventeen-year-old bride. "We should encourage Roscoe and Iola to marry, now that they are free. I suspect they harbor some affection from their years together at Mother Grubb's house."

"To think I once believed her to be a kindly woman," Callie mentioned.

"No matter who marries whom, I am glad to know neither your father nor your brother has plans to kill us. All's well that ends well," Tristan said, quoting the Bard of Avon, a far better writer than Horace Walpole.

"Not exactly," Gareth replied. "There is one more thing that wants doing. Callie has been concerned about her sister feeling she will always be inferior. I know you have struggled with the same emotion, Tris. We have resolved to share all with you equally except our mates and will quarter the year alternating the use of our titles with you. You may go to London for half the season in our name and be lord and lady of the manor for six months of the year since no one can tell us apart."

Clio brightened and hugged her twin. "You are the most generous of sisters!"

But Tristan frowned. "I will always bear the brand that says I am number two if anyone wants to expose us."

"Not after today. Follow me." Gareth rose and took a puzzled Callie by the hand. They descended the tower stairs and made their way to the dungeon.

There Oskar stood by a brazier filled with hot coals. The branding iron with the number II glowed red in its midst. Without hesitation, Gareth stripped to the waist and exposed his shoulder to his steward. Callie threw herself across his naked back. "I never asked this of you, only that we share."

"Yes, milord, I am loath to carry out your orders. Miss Finch might never forgive me." Oskar held his large hands tightly clenched behind his back.

"I order you to make me the same as my twin, Oskar." Gently, Gareth set his little wife aside.

"No, this is too much!" Tristan protested. "You do not know the pain you will suffer. I admit I have been jealous at times, but never wanted this."

"You were a boy. I am a man and will endure it. Once I stood by as our father branded you the lesser twin. Now we will be equal again. Apply the brand, Oskar."

Clio, speechless for a change, wrapped Callie in her arms as her twin could not watch. Even she closed her eyes as the scent and sizzle roasting meat filled the dungeon. Gareth released not a scream but a moan so extended it might have issued from a soul in Hell. He fell to his knees and was uplifted by his brother who helped him up the secret stairs to the solar which served as the bedchamber of the marquess and his bride with Clio and Tristan sleeping above. There a basin of cold water and unguents waited to soothe the wound. Gareth lay on his stomach on the bed while Oskar bathed the wound, applied the grease and bandages.

"My guess is I will be sleeping on my stomach for quite a few nights," Gareth managed to jest. Though she had managed to stay on her feet throughout the ordeal, Callie now sank, weak-kneed, onto the bed beside him.

"Don't you dare swoon now, Calliope Longleigh," Clio said vehemently.

"My dear sister, even for us this was simply too gothic." Callie closed her eyes and allowed herself to drift away.

Twenty-eight

At Almack's little had changed in the absence of the twins. The hall remained crowded, the music still excelled, and the refreshments continued to be inadequate. With all the feathers in her coiffure quivering like a nervous cockatoo, the Lady Patroness inclined her head toward Liza Mallet and discretely covered her lips with a fan.

"However do they do it, the Longleighs create scandal then emerge from it simply shining? We barred their unruly daughters from our activities and now here is one of them back again holding the title of Marchioness of Blackwater and decked out in a quantity of jewels worth far more than a crop of wool. I wanted to turn the marquess and his bride away, but backed as they were by the Duke and Duchess of Bellevue who assured me they only wanted to listen to the music to help deal with their grief, I could hardly do as I wished. It would have seemed small of me."

Her mean little eyes stared at the young couple dressed in black who sat quietly away from the dancing and accepted condolences on the death of the former Viscount Marston's father while at the same time assuming their new roles of marquess and marchioness. The new Lady Blackwater held her head crowned with a stunning ruby tiara rather regally. Young women who approached her in awe of her achievement asked to see the matching ring she bore on one small finger.

Evidently, Clarissa had kept mum about the events at Castle Blackwater, confiding not even in her inquisitive aunt. Lady Mallet's hands ceased to sweat inside her long kid gloves. She had no doubt that young lady could and would spread tales as she had threatened if Liza attempted to tell the bizarre truth of their stay. James Longleigh had escaped the marital mousetrap and fled. She must put a good face on the matter and consider it closed.

"I do believe the Hardacre brothers must have reached an agreement with Bellevue before we journeyed to the castle. It seems obvious now that Clarissa, Angelique, and myself were invited along only to fill out the house party. Take my word upon it, that title and estate is no great achievement. The castle is crude as was the late marquess, a foul man unlamented. Why, Angelique has stated she would never again wish to visit such a place, let alone live there permanently. Oh, my best wishes on the engagement of Clarissa to Chester Buckley. May they experience every happiness."

The crest of feathers ruffled again in agitation as the Lady Patroness nodded. "I suppose 'twas the best the poor child could do. She possesses neither great fortune nor beauty and has far, far too much intellect. If ever a woman was meant to sit in the corner and spin out the rest of her life it was Clarissa. Her mother is resigned to the match, which is better than none. At least, my niece will have a decent roof over her head, and Chester is third in line for the title if Blandon and his son should die. One never knows whom fortune will fancy."

"Quite, though it always seems to favor the Longleighs," Lady Mallet said with bitterness. "However, since those pestilential twins have married—and yes, I did witness the nuptials performed in a church with a proper priest, though I did not see the special license, Blandon has turned his eyes toward my daughter. Since our stay at the castle, she has begun to appreciate that life with a less than dashing widower might be more to her taste. Angelique will be under no pressure to produce an heir as Blandon has one in the nursery, but I fear her offspring will push the title further away from Chester and your niece."

"Do not give it any more thought. I doubt such an odd couple will reproduce in any great amount, though I must say they seem happy in their choice. I have never seen Chester looking less hangdog. Just look at them romping around the dance floor together."

Both ladies took a moment to study Chester and Clarissa as they passed nearby. Clarissa defiantly wore her spectacles and though much less clumsy because of that, still managed to stumble against her intended, putting a big grin on his wide face as he set her to rights again. They exuded a carefree joy few in the room seemed to share.

Lady Mallet turned her attention to Angelique who danced with Lord Blandon, his heated blue eyes ever on her bosom rather than her beautiful face which bore a stiff smile. "Yes, Angelique is making progress, I do think," she confided. "Still, it does rankle that Calliope Longleigh will always have precedence over her even when my daughter becomes a countess."

The Lady Patroness, suffering from the same affliction of vision as Clarissa, squinted her beady black eyes at the Blackwater couple. "If that *is* Calliope Longleigh and the former Viscount Marston. How shall we ever know?"

~ * ~

The Duchess of Bellevue made use of her always present and ever handy fan to cool herself after a vigorous set of dances with her recuperated husband. She, too, eyed her daughter and her new husband with a sharp gray stare. Under the cover of the music and the thumping of feet, she said to her spouse, "You do realize that is Clio and not Callie. Only Clio would want to thumb her nose at the Lady Patroness by appearing here with a new title and in all her finery, and Callie would be twisting a curl by now. Still, Clio could not resist the temptation to wear her signature color in red gems when she should have worn jet or onyx while in mourning. Others might catch on to the situation."

"Then you believe Callie and the real marquess remain at Castle Blackwater because he has injured his shoulder," Bellevue replied.

"It is very hard to tell what I believe at this moment, but yes on that particular matter. Obviously, the new marquess was not up to a trip to London and allowed his brother and sister-in-law to take their place. How generous of him." She raised her fan higher partly to cover their conversation and also to cool her husband so recently sick she did not want him overheated, at least not on the dance floor.

"But most irregular."

"As if anything about this affair has been normal. James claimed the twins eloped by means of a secret passage in the castle and hid in a bawdyhouse while their grooms arranged for the wedding. Only his resourcefulness in escaping his locked room and hunting them down prevented old Lord Blackwater from taking advantage of them there. He could hardly make up a more outrageous story. I think he was also candid in saying that Blackwater fell from a window during their duel and later died of his injuries. I have given out the story about the fall from a horse and that we sent James along to negotiate the marriages since you were too ill to do so. Supposedly, neither of our girls wanted an elaborate wedding. Think of all the money you saved and not about the circumstances."

Bellevue looked at his wife with great admiration. "That seems true enough, or they would not have eloped, and I was certainly not up to killing anyone to preserve their honor or forcing those boys to the altar as I had to do with Iris' husband. Still, if those young men ever make our twins girls unhappy, I will make sure our daughters are widowed." He cast a very feral grin in the direction of his latest son-in-law who noted it and paled a little.

"Stop that, Pearce!" The duchess gave her husband a light whack with the fan. "Everything worked out entirely well as I felt it might in the end. I managed to get Clarissa Downey a husband, also," the duchess said rather smugly. "It seems as if Angelique will accept Lord Blandon shortly now that James has fled."

"Taking credit for that also, are we?" The duke let loose with one of his great basso laughs and turned heads.

His small wife rapped him on the arm again a little harder. "Not so loud! Yes, I do take credit for those marriages as well. If Blandon had not been attracted into the twins' circle, I doubt neither he nor Chester would have bothered with the other girls. In a way, I introduced and encouraged them all by bringing round the Hardacre boys who provided some healthy competition."

"I am not so sure healthy is the word I would use about our daughters switching places at will. I must see they raise a manor house so we can visit them comfortably. Staying at an ancient castle in Scotland for the hunting and fishing is one thing, but bedding without privacy in a great hall is quite another."

"I understand they have already acquired property that might serve as a guesthouse or be torn down to raise a manor with easy access to both the castle and a charming beach."

"That won't make their living arrangements any less than irregular."

"No more irregular than a duke who dances and sleeps with his own wife," Lady Flora chided with a fond smile sent her husband's way.

"And adores her. You forgot that, my darling." The duke produced a tender grin quite the opposite of the ones he used on sons-in-law.

"I never forget that. If my twins are as fortunate, they may run their household in any way they see fit."

"As if we could stop them," the duke answered, slipping his arm around her waist. "No need to chaperone a married couple now that we've gotten them in the door of this utterly boring place. Shall we leave and take our pleasures at home?"

"As soon as the carriage can get us there."

Meet Lynn Shurr

Lynn Shurr grew up in Pennsylvania Dutch country but left to wander the world shortly after getting a degree in English literature. After living in several states and Europe, she picked up a degree in librarianship. Her first reference job brought her to the Cajun Country of Louisiana. Eventually, she became director of a library system. For her, the old saying, "Once you've tasted bayou water, you will always remain here," came true. She raised three children near the banks of the Bayou Teche and lives there still with her astronomer husband where she writes, paints, and studies history

Other Works From The Pen Of
Lynn Shurr

Lady Flora's Rescue: ***Book One of the Longleigh Chronicles***. - Lady Flora follows the man she loves into the American wilderness not knowing he plans to remain there. Will he choose love over his own
liberty?

The Perfect Daughter: ***Book Two of the Longleigh Chronicles***. - When a fascinating gentleman rejects perfection, what must a young lady do to gain his love? Perhaps, seduction.

Daughter of the Rainbow, Book Three of the Longleigh Chronicles. – Shy but lovely Iris Longleigh is passionate about only two things—painting and Lord Valls, who will not marry her due to a secret he harbors.

A Taste of Bayou Water - a prequel to *Blessings and Curses*. When Celine Landry refuses to leave Cajun Country to marry billionaire Jonathan Hartz, what else can a brilliant techno-geek do but try to become Cajun?

Blessings and Curses - Adrienne and Pete—is their love real or are they the victims of an old traiteur's love potion?

The Courville Rose - Can four souls find love in two bodies?

A Place Apart - A wounded warrior and a society girl both seek seclusion on the same deserted island. Sparks fly!

Letter to Our Readers

Enjoy this book?

You can make a difference

As an independent publisher, Wings ePress, Inc. does not have the financial clout of the large New York Publishers. We can't afford large magazine spreads or subway posters to tell people about our quality books.

But, we do have something much more effective and powerful than ads. We have a large base of loyal readers.

Honest Reviews help bring the attention of new readers to our books.

If you enjoyed this book, we would appreciate it if you would spend a few minutes posting a review on the site where you purchased this book or on the Wings ePress, Inc. webpages at: https://wingsepress.com/

Visit Our Website

For The Full Inventory
Of Quality Books:

Wings ePress.Inc
https://wingsepress.com/

Quality trade paperbacks and downloads
in multiple formats,
in genres ranging from light romantic comedy
to general fiction and horror.
Wings has something for every reader's taste.
Visit the website, then bookmark it.
We add new titles each month!

Wings ePress Inc.
3000 N. Rock Road
Newton, KS 67114